Thea had a
Joe as a hus

Doing all the th
his wife, and she
shockingly powerful appeal.

But Joe? Good old Joe, her childhood friend and
confidant, the guiding star of her teenage years?
Joe, who had never turned her away no matter
how irritating she'd become?

Yes. Dear God, yes.

There was only one small drawback—Joe saw
her as his sister, and nothing else.

Caroline Anderson's nursing career was brought to an abrupt halt by a back injury, but her interest in medical things led her to work first as a medical secretary, and then, after completing her teacher training, as a lecturer in Medical Office Practice to trainee medical secretaries. She lives in rural Suffolk with her husband, two daughters, mother and assorted animals.

Recent titles by the same author:

THE IDEAL CHOICE
THE REAL FANTASY
ONE STEP AT A TIME
TENDER TOUCH
AND DAUGHTER MAKES THREE
THAT'S MY BABY!
A FAMILIAR STRANGER

IF YOU NEED ME. . .

BY

CAROLINE ANDERSON

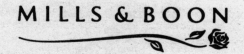

MILLS & BOON

First published in Great Britain 1997
Harlequin Mills & Boon Limited,
Eton House, 18-24 Paradise Road, Richmond, Surrey TW9 1SR

© Caroline Anderson 1997

ISBN 0 263 80014 8

Set in Times 10 on 12 pt. by
Rowland Phototypesetting Limited
Bury St Edmunds, Suffolk

03-9702-44952-D

Printed and bound in Great Britain
by Mackays of Chatham PLC, Chatham

CHAPTER ONE

'IF YOU need me,' he'd said, 'promise you'll just shout. Wherever I am, whatever I'm doing, I'll be there for you. You only have to ask.'

Well, she'd promised, and she certainly needed him now. Drawing a steadying breath and brushing the unruly tangle of brown curls back off her face, she approached the receptionist.

'I'd like to see Mr Armitage, please. I understand he's got a clinic today.'

The woman regarded Thea with a total lack of curiosity. 'Well—yes, he has, but he's fully booked, I'm afraid. Do you have a letter from your GP? He ought to write really, and we'll send you an appointment—unless it's very urgent?'

Thea shook her head. 'No—I'm sorry. I just wanted a quick word with him. I'll wait until he's free.'

The receptionist looked at Thea patiently as if she were a rather dense child. 'He won't see you without a letter or an appointment.'

'Then I'd better make an appointment for the end of his clinic.'

The woman shook her head. 'Not without a letter.'

Thea sighed. Damned efficiency. This woman had turned it into an art form! 'Could you just tell him I'm here and let him make the decision about whether or not

he'll see me?' she said sweetly. 'The name's Thea
Stow—Thea Reynolds.'

'Take a seat,' the receptionist said heavily, and went
out of the back door of her office, disappearing into the
bowels of the clinic. Thea sat—not out of obedience but
sheer exhaustion. She hadn't slept for three nights, the
journey from Bristol had been horrendous and she was
unable to shake off the terrible lassitude that suddenly
overwhelmed her. Lassitude and fear. What if she
couldn't get to see him tonight? What if he went home?
She didn't know his address—

'Mrs Stow?'

She lifted her head.

The receptionist gave her a chilly smile. 'He said he'll
make an exception if you could wait till the end of his
clinic, but he'll only be able to give you a moment.'

She nodded. 'Thank you. How long will the
clinic last?'

'About another couple of hours or so, I expect—if
he's not called out. He's a very busy man.' It was said
with disapproval, as if Thea were going to waste his
valuable time unforgivably.

'I'm sure he is busy,' Thea murmured. Two hours.
Her back ached, her leg was cramping periodically and
she just wanted to lie down. She glanced around at the
other women in the clinic. At least she blended in, she
thought with a wry grin, and then her back twinged again
and the grin slipped, just as a nurse came by.

The woman's friendly smile was her undoing. She felt
the helpless tears well up again, and she turned away. A
second later a gentle hand touched her shoulder. 'Are
you all right, my love?'

She sniffed and brushed the tears off her cheeks. 'I'm sorry. I'm just tired. I'm waiting to see Mr Armitage.'

'Oh, dear, he's on the drag, too. Come with me; I'll make you a cup of tea and see if we can't jump the queue a bit. What's your name?'

'Thea,' she said wearily, almost overwhelmed by the kindness. 'Thea Stow.' She stood up awkwardly, and the nurse took her bag and put an arm round her shoulders.

'How much longer have you got to go?'

Thea's hand came down and rested protectively over the swollen curve of her abdomen. 'Just under four weeks,' she said.

'Not long, then. I expect you'll be glad when it's all over.'

Over? Thea thought. It would be just beginning. At first she had been delighted. Now she just felt terribly alone and afraid. The nurse ushered her into a cubicle, told her to pop up on the couch and draped a blanket over her. 'I'll get you that tea, and then we'll see if we can't hurry the boss along a bit.'

Thea leant against the backrest and closed her eyes. It was wonderful to lie down. If she was left here for long enough in this quiet little room she might just doze off—

'Do we have any notes?'

Thea's eyes flew open just as the door swung inwards and a tall man swept in, white coat flapping, stethoscope dangling round his neck.

'Apparently not. She's been fitted in,' one of his entourage explained.

A quick frown marred the familiar features, and then the man looked up at her and his eyes widened.

'Thea?'

'Hello, Joe,' she said softly, and to her chagrin her eyes filled again and the hated tears splashed over onto her cheeks.

He recovered his composure before she did, and turned to his colleagues.

'Would you give us a moment, please?'

They faded away, and the next second she was in his arms, her head cradled protectively against his chest while the tears leaked out and soaked his shirt-front. 'Oh, Tink,' he murmured, and the old familiar endearment just made it worse. She gulped noisily and wondered with the last remnant of thought why she wasn't one of those Hollywood heroines who could cry delicately.

Finally she pulled out of his arms and sagged against the backrest. 'Sorry,' she mumbled. 'I'm just tired, and it's so good to see you—' The tears welled again, and she swore softly and blew her pink nose on the tissue he handed her.

Then she looked up into those beautiful grey-blue eyes that had seen her through so many scrapes and a wobbly smile edged its way out, accompanied by a sniff.

She was rewarded by an answering smile that held years of affection. 'That's my girl. Now, how about telling me what's going on? The last time I saw you was— oh, years ago.'

'Three, at my father's funeral.' She twisted the soggy tissue and it disintegrated. 'That's why I'm here. You said if I ever needed anything I should come and find you.'

His eyes flicked down, over the bump under the blanket, and back to her face. 'And you have.'

She nodded. 'Yes.'

His hand squeezed her. 'This is obviously going to take some time, and I've got my clinic to deal with. Can you hang on? Then I'll take you home and we can have a long chat. Are you on your own here?'

She nodded again. 'Yes.'

'I'll get a nurse to bring you a cup of tea. Are you comfortable on that couch? You could stay here if you like, have a little doze. You look exhausted.'

'I am.' She couldn't summon an answering smile, and with a muttered oath he dropped a kiss on her forehead and left her there, with a promise to be back as quickly as he could.

The nurse came with a cup of tea and instructions from Joe to check Thea over and make sure everything was all right. She took her blood pressure and listened to the baby's heartbeat and then straightened with a smile. 'You'll do. Have that cuppa and a little zizz, and he'll be back to see you in a while. I'll make sure you aren't disturbed.'

The door closed softly behind her, and after finishing her tea Thea settled back against the pillows and tried to relax. It was impossible. Until now her only thought had been to find Joe and get here. Now she was here, and it suddenly dawned on her that she was going to have to explain everything to him, and that would be complicated. There was so much to say, so much to tell him, so many painful memories to wade through. Where should she start? She was so tired now—so bone-weary that even to talk was too much effort.

She needn't have worried. He came back into the room some time later and gave her a thoughtful look.

'Where are you staying tonight?' he asked.

She blinked. She hadn't got that far yet in her own mind.

'I don't know.'

'Have you come up from Bristol alone?'

She turned away. Sympathy now would finish her. 'Yes,' she told him. Just the one word, said flatly, and with no hint of the tragedy it concealed.

'Then stay with me. Have a good night's sleep and we'll talk tomorrow. I'll take the morning off—if it'll keep that long?'

Her smile was fragile. 'It'll keep, but won't your wife mind?'

'I don't have a wife,' he answered. 'Or a significant other. Only the cat, and he'll have to lump it.'

The smile steadied a little, her anxiety receding another notch. 'Oh,' she said. 'That would be wonderful. Thank you.'

He twitched the blanket off her. 'Don't thank me— you haven't tasted my cooking yet.'

She chuckled, some of the tension draining away already. 'You look well enough on it—or does the hospital kitchen make up the shortfall?'

He laughed softly. 'You guessed. Right, let's take you home and feed you. When did you last eat, talking of looking well or not?'

She shrugged. 'I'm not sure. This morning, perhaps?' It was a lie. She hadn't eaten since lunchtime the previous day, and that had been a stale sandwich. Suddenly her stomach rumbled, and he tutted and helped her to her feet and into her coat, tucking it round her chin.

'It's cold out,' he said, and she wasn't sure if it was her imagination or if his voice sounded a little gruff. He opened the door and ushered her out, then down the corridor to the end and out into the car park. The receptionist was still at her station and blinked, visibly eaten by curiosity. Thea resisted the urge to thumb her nose. It would have required too much energy. Instead she concentrated on putting one foot in front of the other and making her way to the car.

'How did you get here?' Joe asked as he settled her in the passenger seat. 'Is your car in the car park?'

'No. No car. I walked from the station.'

His brow creased but he made no comment, although she sensed that he was clamping his jaw against yet another question. He slid behind the wheel, slammed his door and started the engine, then pulled out into the evening traffic. It was dark, some time after five, and the traffic was heavy. Thea leant against the headrest and let the car's gentle motion lull her.

It lulled her very effectively. The next thing she was aware of was Joe's hand on her shoulder, shaking her slightly, his voice soft. 'Thea? Come on, sweetheart; time to get out of the car. We're here.'

She turned towards him and sighed sleepily, and then found herself scooped up as if she weighed nothing, her head lolling against his shoulder, his broad chest firm against her body as he carried her effortlessly into the house.

She was dimly aware of warmth and peace, and feeling enormously safe, and then she slid into oblivion again.

'I suppose you want to know what's happened?'

His mouth quirked. 'Because you turn up at the hospital out of the blue, three years after I last saw you, eight months pregnant and looking as if the world has come to an end? I must confess to a certain curiosity.'

She returned his gentle smile, then her expression faltered. 'I don't know where to start.'

'How about the beginning.'

Her smile was weary. They were sitting in the kitchen, a pile of hot buttered toast on the table between them, drinking their second cup of tea. At least, it was her second. Joe might have been up for ages.

Thea took a deep breath and let it out slowly. 'The beginning. OK. His name was Mike Stow; he was a patient of mine when I was doing my neurology rotation. He asked me out, and I said I couldn't go because I was involved with his case. Two weeks later I moved on to A and E and he contacted me again. I went out with him, and we had a lot of fun. I didn't think it would hurt. After all, I knew it wouldn't be for long, because he had an inoperable brain tumour and it was just a matter of time.'

She twisted her wedding ring absently. 'The tumour was like the little girl that had a little curl—when it was good it was very, very good, and he felt great. At other times it was bad, and—well, he would black out and have agonising headaches and then he'd be low for days. It was awful, watching him and knowing what was happening. He was haunted by this insidious thing growing inside him. He said he could feel the tentacles tightening round his mind.'

Joe squeezed her hand, and she looked up and met his sympathetic eyes. 'He asked me to marry him. Everybody thought I was crazy because he was so ill, but it made it easier really. It was the only thing I could really give him.

'Anyway, we got married very quietly, about a year ago. He got much worse shortly afterwards, and I knew he wouldn't be alive for long. Then one week he seemed to rally, and we went away for the weekend. It was wonderful. The weather was beautiful—the gods loved him, he said. Then we came home and three days later he went into a coma. He never recovered. He died in the hospice at the beginning of June.'

She looked down at her hands, surprised to see Joe's fingers twined round her own, the knuckles white. 'Did he know about the baby?' he asked softly.

She shook her head. 'No. I conceived during that last weekend. I—it had been some time since he'd felt that well. It caught us both by surprise, I think.'

'And he wasn't on any drugs?'

She shook her head again. 'No. He refused to take anything stronger than paracetamol unless it was really bad. If he'd been on drugs he probably would have been sterile. Anyway, for a while things jostled along in the way they do, and then all of a sudden everything fell apart. His life assurance had lapsed apparently, and so the mortgage was in arrears with no hope of it being paid off. The building society repossessed the house, sold it at a loss and I was left with nothing. I found a flat and moved in, and then last week the landlord realised I was pregnant and chucked me out. They had a no-children rule, he said, and I was about to break that rule.'

'So you came to find me.'

She met his eyes and wondered if her own were as revealing. 'Yes,' she said flatly. 'I had nowhere else to go.' She looked down, away from the sympathy and concern that would be the end of her composure. 'I want to ask you a favour. I'd like you to lend me enough money to rent a flat and support me and the baby for six months. Then I'll get a job and pay you back. It'll take time, of course—'

'No.'

'I must pay you back!'

'No,' he said again. 'There won't be any need to pay me back, because I'm not going to lend you any money.'

Her heart seemed to stop for a moment, then start again with a thud. Panic washed over her, threatening to submerge her. She looked up at him, frantic. 'Joe—you said you'd help me—'

'And so I shall, but not by saddling you with debt. You can live here. The house is plenty big enough. You can pay for your keep by cooking something other than TV dinners for me in the evening, and by keeping me company when I get home from work.' His mouth tipped in a grin. 'It'll be nice to' have someone to talk to, and if I recall we always managed to talk.'

'I used to talk. You used to listen. As *I* recall, I drove you mad.'

He laughed. 'Only a little, and I'm sure your conversation has matured a shade in twenty years! Anyway, that's my offer. Take it or leave it.'

She looked into his eyes, searching them for any sign of doubt or hesitation, but she found none. 'I'll take it,' she said softly. 'I have no choice, Joe. And you're right. It will be nice to have someone to talk to. Thank you.'

She looked down, her eyes suddenly filling again, and his hands cupped hers, huge and protective, swallowing her little fingers whole in his fists. 'You'll need baby equipment. May I give it to you, as a present?'

She gulped. 'I won't need much.'

He laughed shortly. 'Cobblers,' he said bluntly. 'I've never yet seen a baby that could travel light.'

Thea's answering smile was weak. The cost of her baby equipment had been something she had tried to avoid thinking about. To have the worry taken off her shoulders at a stroke seemed too good to be true.

'We'll see,' she told him now, intending to spend the next few days looking through small ads for second-hand bargains. Joe, however, apparently had other ideas.

'How are you feeling now?' he asked.

'Fine. Much better.'

'Good. Let's go out now and look at things,' he said, and, taking her cup out of her hand, he tipped the dregs down the sink, swept the last slice of cold, soggy toast into the bin and hustled her out of the kitchen. 'Two minutes,' he told her.

'I need make-up,' she protested, and he rolled his eyes.

'You do not need make-up. You look lovely.'

'I look,' she told him bluntly, 'like the wreck of the Hesperus, but you're very sweet to pretend you hadn't noticed. Five minutes.'

He sighed. 'Five, then, but no more. I have to go to work this afternoon and there's a lot to buy.'

He took her to a specialist baby shop and asked the assistant what a new baby would need.

'Oh, all sorts,' she told him. 'We have a list. Where do you want to start?'

'At the top?' he suggested. 'Perhaps if you could jot down the things we decide on, and then they could all be delivered together?'

The list was frighteningly long. Thea's eyes widened,

but Joe didn't turn a hair, and she didn't like to argue in
public. She'd have to find a way to stop him before he
went too far, though, she realised.

However, he didn't give her a chance, and it dawned
on her that he would ignore her no matter how vociferous
her protest.

Oh, well, she would have to make a note of how much
it all came to and pay him back in the future. She just
hoped he didn't go too mad and have the entire contents
of the shop delivered to his house!

Almost, but not quite. He was comfortingly discerning,
asking what was necessary, what was desirable and what
was superfluous, and because the assistant had children
herself she was able to make helpful suggestions.

She showed them prams and buggies, cots, carry-cots,
cribs and accessories. They looked at clothes, discussed
sizing and how many of each size would be necessary,
talked about terry versus disposable nappies and whether
Thea would breast- or bottle-feed.

She felt colour brush her cheeks. 'Um—I hope to
breast-feed,' she mumbled, acutely aware of Joe so close
behind her.

'So you'll only need a few bottles for water, juice and
so on. You'll still need a sterilising unit, though—this
is a good one.'

The subject safely negotiated, Thea sighed with relief
and followed the woman on to the next phase—toys.

'I think toys could wait for a week or two,' she began,
but was overruled.

'How about a mobile over the cot? Something colourful that plays a soothing lullaby?'

So the mobile went on the list, and the activity centre

that screwed to the side of the cot, and a play mat that doubled as a changing mat and carry bag.

Then Joe started on her. 'How about clothes?' he asked. 'You'll need something comfy to slop around in afterwards, and nighties for hospital, and special underwear—'

'Why don't you leave us to it for half an hour?' the assistant suggested, seeing Thea's embarrassment. Joe conceded with visible reluctance, and Thea suppressed a smile. Nothing changed, she thought fondly. He'd always organised her—probably always would, if she gave him a chance.

The assistant ushered her upstairs to the maternity-wear department, and together they looked at bras with apparently infinite adjustment, which would offer good support until the end of her pregnancy and would double as nursing bras for afterwards.

'They're pretty too,' the assistant said with a smile, 'so your husband will appreciate them as well.'

Thea lost her smile. 'Um—he's not my husband. He's my brother—sort of. I'm a widow.'

'But I thought—' The assistant's composure crumbled, her face stricken with remorse and sympathy. 'Oh, dear, how sad. I am so sorry. Oh, what a dreadful thing. . .'

Thea forced a smile. 'It's all right, really. I'm used to it now. And it will be nice to have pretty underwear, even if it's just me that gets to enjoy it.'

The assistant was a darling, Thea decided. Not much older than Thea herself, she nevertheless mothered and mollycoddled her through the trying-on process, and Thea felt so awful for distressing her that she allowed herself to be talked into endless purchases.

Finally they rejoined Joe downstairs, and the assistant totted up the list of apparently urgently necessary items that Joe had selected and gave him a staggering total.

'Joe, that's ridiculous!' Thea protested breathlessly, but he just smiled that implacable smile and handed over a credit card.

'When can you deliver the items?' he asked.

'Tomorrow, if you're local. The buggy will take a week, but everything else is in stock now.'

'Excellent.' With a big smile for the assistant, Joe ushered the still stunned Thea out into the shopping arcade.

She turned to him, mouth open to protest, and met those calm, enigmatic blue-grey eyes. 'Don't say it, Thea,' he said softly. 'After all your parents did for me it's little enough. I seem to remember coming to you with not much more than the clothes I stood up in.'

'That's different,' she began, but he shook his head.

'No, Thea, it's no different. It just gives me a chance, twenty years later, to balance the books. Now, no more arguing, there's a good girl, and we'll go home and look at the bedrooms and decide which one to turn into a nursery, and then after lunch I'll have to leave you, I'm afraid, because I'm operating this afternoon. Still, you'll be OK, won't you?'

She gave up fighting. He was so kind, so concerned, so genuinely generous that she had to forgive him for being overbearing and manipulative. His motives, after all, were the best. 'I'll be fine,' she assured him with a fond smile.

*   *   *

Thea was exhausted. The shopping trip this morning had been necessary but a little soon after her wearing journey and the hell of the preceding weeks. Still, she felt happier now everything was organised, and the room beside her own that Joe had said she could use as a nursery was wonderful. It was decorated in pretty peaches and greens, and it had a communicating door through to the bathroom off her bedroom, which would be very useful for the inevitable bathing and cleaning-up operations.

She made herself a cup of tea and then wandered through the house, familiarising herself with the geography and also, coincidentally, with Joe's taste.

It was a lovely house, probably built in the thirties, and it was on the outskirts of a little village, set quietly down a country lane and yet only three miles from the hospital and the town.

Decorated in pale, sunny yellows and gentle blues, the softest jade and warm terracotta, the house reflected a mature and discerning taste that was completely in accord with her own. It was a very big house for a single man, though, and she wondered if there had been someone on the scene when he had bought it—or if he had someone in mind now.

On second thoughts, perhaps he'd just wanted something large and solid to call his own. He had always been territorial. Losing everything so young had done that to him. His bedroom had always been sacrosanct, only Thea ever allowed in there, and then only by invitation.

She found herself in his bedroom now; it was much bigger than his room at her parents' house had been, but still very much his. It was a little untidy—a shirt hung over the back of a chair, a tie dropped on the bed, the quilt rumpled where he had sat to tie his shoes, she guessed. A group of silver-framed pictures on a chest of drawers caught her eye.

She went over to them, and found that she was looking at herself, at a much younger Thea—perhaps eight or nine—standing next to her parents and Joe, then sixteen and gangling as only adolescent boys could gangle.

There were other pictures, of her mother in the garden, her father sitting at the wheel of the ancient Bentley that had been his pride and joy, and one that she remembered from his other bedroom, a rather battered photo of Joe with his parents, taken shortly before they died.

Joe had been twelve, and of the three years between then and his coming to live with her parents he had said nothing. She'd known he had been with an uncle, but beyond that nothing had ever been said—at least not to her, and she had had the intelligence not to ask. Getting Joe in a temper was not to be undertaken lightly.

She smiled at the memory and let her eyes stray over the other photos. There was another one of her, at her graduation, shortly before her father had died. He must have sent it to Joe. How strange that Joe should have it framed and displayed in his bedroom.

Still, she supposed she was the only 'family' he had left now, apart from the uncle nobody talked about. She wondered if he would ever tell her what had gone on in those three painful years.

She went back downstairs, her back aching, and, fetching another cup of tea, she settled herself in the sitting room, put her feet up on the wonderfully comfy sofa and watched birds feeding from a net of peanuts hanging outside the French windows. She had company, in the form of Sylvester, Joe's rather fine black and white cat. He also found the birds fascinating. Thea wondered what he would make of the baby, and then wondered how Joe himself would cope with the inevitable disruption and chaos that a new baby would bring.

Would it be the end of a beautiful friendship? Lord, she hoped not. She'd have to keep out of his way as much as possible—not that it would be that difficult if he was working long hours. She'd have to cook something for them for tonight, after she'd had a few minutes of shut-eye now, she decided, and snuggled down in the chair.

The cat, seeing a perfect opportunity, jumped up and settled himself on her lap, and she laid a hand on his head and scratched his ear. The purrs shook her legs, and with a sleepy smile she closed her eyes and let her head fall back against the cushions.

She looked exhausted. Joe shed his tie, tossed it over the banisters, kicked off his shoes and then went silently back into the sitting room. He sat opposite her and watched her sleeping, the cat curled contentedly on her lap, hardly bothering to open an eye to acknowledge his presence.

What hell had she been through this year? To meet this Mike and fall in love, knowing he was dying, and then to marry him knowing she was condemning herself to yet more suffering—not that the Thea he had known could have done anything else. She was as soft as putty, kind and generous and impulsive.

He was surprised she had made it as a doctor. He would have thought the suffering she'd encountered would have torn her apart, but apparently not.

And now she was pregnant, homeless and destitute.

No, not homeless. She would have a home with him for as long as she needed it. No way would his little Tinkerbell be out on the streets. She had been the one bright thing in his life at fifteen, the only thing that had kept him on the rails. She had literally saved his life one night, coming into his bedroom and sitting on the bed and chattering to him happily about what had gone on at school, and he had clenched his fist around the handful of sleeping tablets he had stolen from her mother and listened to her babbling, and had wondered if she would ever go away and let him get on with what he had to do.

Her mother had called and she had slid off the bed; then, halfway to the door, she had come back and shyly slipped her arms round his neck.

'I love you, Joe,' she whispered to him, and he sat there staring at the door she had closed behind her and thought what his death would do to her. He couldn't do it, not after that, so he went into the bathroom and flushed the tablets down the loo.

He wondered, in the emptiness of the days that followed, if he had done the right thing, and then he would see her skipping around in the garden, head flung back in a wild tangle of nut-brown curls, her eyes wide and trusting like those of a fawn and yet touched with mischief, and he knew she would have seen his death as a betrayal of her friendship.

It was a turning point in his life, that realisation. Someone actually needed him, even if that someone was an irritating, bouncy, butterfly-minded child of seven. He began, bit by bit, to open up to her, to give her something of himself in return for her devotion, and slowly, bit by bit, her love and the kindness and compassion of her parents had thawed the ice around his heart, melted away the agony of the past three years and left him whole again.

Now it was his turn to give something back—something meaningful and necessary to Thea's health and happiness. For the first time in his life someone needed him—not as a doctor but as a friend, a fellow human, as himself.

It was a good feeling.

CHAPTER TWO

THE following day was idyllic for Thea. Joe emptied the room she was to have as a nursery for her baby, and for the tiny clothes gave her a chest of drawers that was just the right height to put the changing mat on. The equipment was all delivered and carried up to the room by the van driver so she could start the unpacking process.

She ignored the nagging backache caused by overdoing things, and by the end of the first day everything was in its place. Just time to make a tasty casserole and pop it in the oven for when Joe came home, she thought.

After the casserole was in the oven she prepared the vegetables, put them on the hob and looked at the chaos. She'd sort it out in a minute. First things first.

She had just sat down in the kitchen with a much needed cup of tea when she heard the swish of tyres on the gravel drive and Joe came in.

He ambled into the kitchen, shedding his tie and jacket, and dropped his hand onto her head, tousling her unruly curls. 'Hi, Tink,' he said with a grin. 'Had a good day?'

She smoothed her hair and gave him a wry smile. 'Lovely. I've put all the baby's things away—the nursery looks lovely.'

'It all came?'.

'Uh-huh. I hope there isn't more!'

He chuckled. 'There will be—there always is. I've

recommended the shop to a couple I saw today—they've just had a nasty surprise. Triplets.'

Thea's eyes widened. 'Triplets?' she squeaked. 'The thought of one is terrifying!'

His smile faded. 'Are you terrified?' he asked gently.

She gave a little shrug. 'No, not really. Not any more; not now I'm here. The variables are becoming fewer. That helps. I know where I'm going to be living for the next few months, I know you'll help me through—that makes so much difference. If you could only know—' She shook her head, unable to express herself, but it wasn't necessary.

Joe understood, as he always understood her. He patted her hand, put the kettle on again and sat down opposite her.

'Where are you going to have the baby?'

She stared at him. 'Where? At your hospital, I suppose—the Audley Memorial. Where else?'

He grinned. 'Where else, indeed? You know I won't be your consultant, though? You'll have to be under one of the others.'

'Of course. I wish you could be, in a way. I trust you.'

He smiled reassuringly at her. 'You can trust my colleagues. I'll get you put under William Parry—he's a good friend of mine. They're all equally professionally adept, but I think you'll get on with William. Anyway, I don't suppose you're anticipating any problems, are you?'

She shook her head. 'No. Everything was quite straightforward at my antenatal checks in Bristol.'

'We ought to get the notes. I'll get my secretary to give them a ring.'

Thea grinned mischievously. '"My secretary", eh? What's it like to be a big-shot consultant, Joe?'

To her amazement he coloured a little. 'Actually it's good,' he admitted with a wry grin, 'but it takes a bit of getting used to. And it can be lonely.'

'Because you're the boss?'

He nodded. 'Exactly. People are naturally a little wary. They watch what they say, and so you don't just walk into a group of people and say, "What's going on, then?" as you might have done before. It would be easy to get paranoid and imagine they were talking about you, if you had a big enough ego.'

His smile didn't hide the uncertainty Thea felt behind his words. So he was lonely. Poor Joe. He'd always been a bit of a loner. She'd assumed it was by choice, but now she began to wonder. Perhaps he naturally distanced himself because he was never sure of his welcome?

'I've cooked supper,' she told him, changing the subject, and his mouth quirked.

'I can tell. There's a wonderful smell drifting from the oven and the kitchen looks a touch used.'

She glanced round. 'I had trouble finding everything. You're not very systematic. And then I was tired so I thought I'd just sit down and have a cup of tea before I cleared it up. And anyway,' she added with a grin, 'you're early.'

'I managed to get away from my clinic promptly, for once, and now I'm going to be punished by having to sort out the kitchen, I suppose.'

She stood up and crossed hastily to the sink, her back aching, her conscience pricking her with guilt. 'I'm sorry. You're right, I've made a dreadful mess—I'll clear it up straight away. Go in the sitting room. I'll bring you a cup of tea—'

'Thea?'

'—when the kettle boils. How do you like it? White, no sugar?' She clattered the pans. 'Or do you want coffee?'

'Tink, shut up.'

She floundered to a halt and swallowed the lump in her throat. 'I'm sorry. It's your house and I'm taking over.'

'Tink, it's your house now too. I was joking. I don't give a damn about the mess. You should see the place when *I* cook!'

His hands were on her shoulders, and he eased her back against his chest and wrapped his arms around her.

'I was teasing you, Thea,' he said softly. 'I always do. Have you forgotten?'

She sniffed back the sudden prickle behind her eyes. 'It's been so long—ages since anybody teased me. The last few weeks there hasn't been much to laugh about. I must have got out of practice. I'm sorry, I'm being silly. Put it down to hormones.'

'Hormones? The last time I put one of your mood swings down to hormones you hit me with a bag full of school-books!'

She giggled. 'You remember that?'

'I'll say. I had a headache for days.'

He turned her gently in his arms and cupped her cheeks in his warm, dry hands. 'It's good to have you around, Tinkerbell. I've missed my little nemesis.'

'I'm not so little now.'

He looked down at her tummy and patted it lightly.

'No. I must say you've lost your figure just a touch— was it something you ate?'

She grinned, a little lopsidedly. 'Fine consultant obstetrician you are!' she teased, pushing his chest so that he stepped away from her, still smiling. 'Cup of tea?'

'Good idea. I'll make it, you sit down. You've probably been overdoing it all day, if I know you. You never did have a grain of sense.'

They swapped understanding smiles, and Thea sat gratefully at the kitchen table and allowed Joe to wait on her. Why not? If it made him feel better, who was she to stop him? She was shattered, anyway, and her legs were aching after all the running around putting the things away upstairs.

'Come and see the nursery,' she said when he had made the tea.

He gave her a keen look. 'Have you really been overdoing it, Thea? You've got to take care of yourself, you know. There's the baby to think about as well.'

'I've been sensible,' she reassured him, and promised herself she would be in future. They went up to the little room and Joe admired all the little things, examined the cot assembly instructions and took them back downstairs to look at while they had tea.

Then, while she cleared up the kitchen and cooked the vegetables to go with the casserole, Joe rolled up his sleeves and disappeared up to the nursery with a screwdriver and the assembly instructions.

The odd muttered curse drifted down the stairs, bringing a smile to her lips, and then she heard his footsteps on the landing.

'Thea? Could you come and hold the end for me?'

She dried her hands and ran up, then held parts and passed bolts and periodically went deaf when he had difficulty and lapsed into Anglo-Saxon, and finally the cot was together, the side went smoothly up and down and Joe stood back, dusted off his hands and grinned at her.

'How about that, then?' he said with pride, and she hugged him and laughed.

'Wonderful. Now all I have to do is put the sheets on and we're ready for off.'

He looked at her bump and then back to her face. 'When are you due?'

'Three and a half weeks.'

He nodded. 'Hmm,' he said.

'Hmm what?'

He shrugged. 'I just wouldn't be surprised if it was early. Have you had a scan?'

She shook her head.

'I'll get you into William's clinic on Monday,' he said thoughtfully. 'Until then, take it easy, eh?'

'Yes, Doctor,' she promised.

He shook his head and laughed. 'Pest. How's supper coming on? I'm starving.'

She did take it easy. All the next day she lolled about, bored out of her mind, and then allowed herself to cook for him. She was going to take a little stroll down the lane but the wind had picked up in the past couple of hours and the sky looked rather menacing, so she decided not to.

Then Joe rang. 'I'll be late tonight—about seven, OK?

I just didn't want you to worry about me. Are you all right?'

'Fine,' she assured him. Bored, but fine. Oh, well. . .

She put the kettle on and sighed. More tea. She'd turn into a teabag at this rate!

Then the power went off.

'Oh, well, I didn't want tea anyway,' she said with a philosophical chuckle, and went into Joe's study. It was a wonderful treasure trove, full of medical textbooks, novels, plays and all sorts.

'Eclectic taste,' Thea decided, and pulled out a textbook on obstetrics. It was the one thing she hadn't yet done in her training for general practice, and would have been her next rotation. She might go back to it after the baby was born. General practice was an area of medicine where women were able to work part-time, and with the baby that would be useful.

She thumbed through the book, and before she knew where she was she was totally absorbed. She settled down in Joe's big, high-backed swivel chair, propped her feet on the edge of the desk and read the book until the light from the window grew too dim.

Still no sign of the power returning, she thought, and got up for a stretch. The wind was still thrashing branches against the windows, and the sky was full of rain that intermittently splattered against the glass, adding to the *Wuthering Heights* atmosphere. She found the sound comforting in a way, and didn't mind at first.

It was later, when the first twinges began, that she started to feel a little threatened by the force of the storm. She rubbed her back absently, staring out over the windswept garden, and wished Joe would come back. It was well after five, the light almost gone, and there was still no power.

She was walking through to the sitting room when the pain hit her. With a little gasp she sagged against the wall and tried to remember her breathing exercises. Gradually the pain eased, and she went back into the kitchen and sat at the table, staring blankly across the dim room. What time was Joe coming home? Seven? Only just over an hour.

She waited, watching the clock, and three minutes later she experienced another strong contraction.

'Three minutes,' she whispered. 'Oh, Lord. Joe, where are you?'

She wondered if she should ring the hospital, and picked up the cordless phone that was lying on the work-top. Nothing. It was mains-operated and dead as a dodo. She hoisted herself to her feet and went into his study, and to her relief there was a conventional phone there. She picked it up and listened for the dialling tone, and found herself staring at the silent instrument through a veil of frustrated tears.

'Damn!' she muttered, and quelled the panic. Joe would be here soon. She was young and healthy, the baby had been fine at the last check-up; she would be perfectly all right.

If only there wasn't this wind—

Another contraction stabbed at her and she sank into his swivel chair with a little cry of alarm. Were they getting stronger, or was it her imagination?

There was a sudden crash in the garden, and she peered out to see that a huge pine tree had fallen across the drive. It could have hit the house, she thought, and terror

gripped her. She was alone, isolated, in the midst of a
storm that threatened to tear the roof off; the phones were
down, the power was off and Joe was missing!

She closed her eyes and forced herself to breathe
deeply and calmly. She was a doctor. She knew what to
do—the theory at least. She would deliver her baby herself, if necessary.

She went upstairs, pausing on the half-landing for
another stabbing contraction, and then made her way into
her bathroom. Shower, she thought, and find a pile of
towels to lay out on the bed.

But the shower was too difficult in the dark, so she
abandoned it, contenting herself with a thorough wash
by hand. She found towels in the airing cupboard on the
landing, by feel rather than sight, and then made her way
into the bedroom.

And now, she thought, settling herself down against
the pillows, we just have to sit back and wait for nature
to get on with it.

Joe turned into the drive and braked sharply, just before
the front of his car ploughed into the fallen tree.

Dear God, what a night! The house was in darkness—
did that mean the power was off, or had Thea just gone
to bed? He pulled in as far as possible so the tail of his
car was off the road, and climbed over the fallen tree.
He hoped she was all right and not too worried by the
wind. He could feel it trying to drag his coat off, and he
ducked his head down and ran for the door.

'Thea?' The house was silent, dark as the grave. He
flicked a light switch fruitlessly. 'Thea? Where are you?'

'Upstairs,' he heard her call, and he dropped his

coat on a chair and ran up two at a time.

'Where?'

'Bedroom.'

He found her huddled in the dark, the quilt pulled up to her chin, shivering. He realised that the house was freezing and the power must have been off for some time.

'Are you all right?' he asked, trying to quell his anxiety.

'I am now,' she told him. 'Joe, I'm in labour, and the phone's not working—' She broke off on a muffled sob, and he pulled her gently into his arms and hugged her.

'You'll be fine. Let me get a torch.'

He felt his way down to the utility room and groped in the drawer for the heavy rubber torch he kept for emergencies. His hand brushed against a candle, and he pulled it out, found a saucer and some matches and went back upstairs.

First he struck a match and lit the candle, then tilted it to dribble wax on the saucer to hold the candle upright. When it was steady he set it near the bed and looked at Thea.

Her face was streaked with tears, and he could tell she had been very frightened. It was a look he recognised well from his work.

'I need to take a look at you,' he told her gently, and, easing back the quilt, he helped her to lie down. Then he went into the bathroom, washed his hands as thoroughly as he could and went back to her. He had no gloves at home, but hopefully he wouldn't be carrying any hospital bugs on his hands.

'I just need to feel your cervix to assess the progress of your labour, Thea,' he told her.

She nodded. 'The contractions are pretty close together,' she told him, and he could tell she was trying to stay calm. 'I think it's moving quite fast.'

'Let's find out,' he murmured, and deftly swept his fingers round the margins of her cervix, checking the shape of the baby's head and the lie—fortunately a straightforward presentation. What he found was both reassuring and yet disturbing, because one thing he was sure of—her baby was coming now, with or without his permission.

'You're almost there, Thea,' he told her calmly. 'Now, the thing is, I daren't risk taking you to hospital in this weather, so I'll try calling the flying squad on my mobile phone from the car.'

'No!' Her fingers latched onto his wrist, surprising him with their strength. 'Don't leave me now!'

'I'm only going downstairs,' he promised, but her grip tightened.

'No—Joe, please! There isn't time. Stay with me!'

He stayed. Her cervix had almost completely dilated, the presentation felt good; there was really no need to call for outside help. He tucked the quilt around her shoulders and sat on the edge of the bed, soothing her through contractions, letting her rest in between, and then she raised her head and looked at him in the flickering candlelight.

'Joe, I want to push,' she said calmly.

'Let me check.'

But she didn't give him time. She drew a deep breath, tucked her chin down and grunted deep in her throat.

He held her hand, wincing at the pressure, and when the contraction died away she threw off the quilt.

'I want to stand up,' she told him. 'I want to walk around.'

She was calm, in control and totally implacable. Joe developed an instant admiration for the midwives who routinely talked women out of crazy ideas when they were in labour. How could they cope? It would drive him to drink.

The next contraction began as her feet hit the floor, and with a gasp she clung to him, hanging on him, her body working hard to expel the baby—the baby he was terrified was going to land on the floor!

'Thea, you can't do this without another person to help me,' he told her. 'Please, Tink, get back on the bed!'

'I'm fine,' she assured him.

He wished he were. His brow was breaking out in a sweat, his hands were damp with fear and for some reason this baby was different from every other one he had ever delivered. Damn her and her independence.

'Kneel, then,' he reasoned, 'but on the bed.' And he helped her up so she lay draped over the headboard and the baby would fall only as far as the mattress.

He pulled a towel under her and checked again, to find that the baby was crowning and would be delivered with the next expulsive effort of her uterus. Damn, it was going so fast. He tried to remember about normal, healthy deliveries and not the problems he was usually called to deal with. What should she do? Something— yes.

'Thea, you'll have to pant now with the next contraction. Do you understand?'

'Mmm,' she mumbled through the headboard. 'I want to push—' Her voice rose in a scream, and he cupped the baby's head and gripped Thea's ankle with his other hand.

'Pant, damn you, pant! Don't push!'

He could hear her panting, her breath ragged and catching on a sob, and then with a slithering splosh the baby was free, falling into his waiting hands and reducing him to putty.

'Easy, now,' he crooned as the baby yelled, and he laid it down and turned Thea so she was lying against the pillows. Then he handed the baby to her, picked up the torch and shone it carefully on the tiny child.

'A boy—oh, Joe—!'

Thea's voice broke, and her hands wrapped lovingly around the tiny body and cradled it against the soft wall of her abdomen.

Joe's chest felt tight, his eyes prickled and he couldn't have spoken to save his life.

Instead he dropped a kiss on Thea's brow, went into the bathroom and washed his hands again to give himself time, then went back and checked that all was well. He had no oxytocin to inject to encourage the placenta to come away, no lights to speak of to see what was going on, no surgical team at the ready if anything went wrong at this stage—Lord, he thought, what if she has a prolapse and her uterus turns inside out? What if she has a postpartum haemorrhage? What if the baby becomes distressed?

It wasn't, not at all. It—or rather he—was suckling peacefully, latched onto Thea's nipple without hesitation, following nature's directions without turning a hair.

He sat down on the edge of the bed with a plop, and looked at Thea in the candlelight. 'How are you?' he asked softly.

She looked up at him, her face radiant in the soft yellow light. 'Wonderful. He's beautiful.'

'He' was bloodstained, his hair was plastered to his tiny scalp and he was pink and wrinkled, but Joe supposed that to Thea he probably was the most wonderful thing in the world.

He swallowed. Damn. How about that? Even he thought the little prune was beautiful. He must be going nuts.

He pulled himself together and remembered his role as midwife, but Thea was fine and would have been fine with or without his help. The placenta came away without problem, was beautifully intact as far as he could tell and Thea was fascinated by it. There was no excessive bleeding, no change in her pulse rate that would indicate haemorrhage, nothing to alarm him at all.

And then, just when he had struggled to check her with the torch to make sure she needed no sutures, the power came back on.

'Just like the flaming cavalry,' he said wryly, and flicked on the light. 'Let's have a look at this young man, then.' He checked the baby swiftly to make sure there were no immediately obvious problems, then wrapped him up again and tucked him in beside Thea.

'I'll bath him when the heating's boosted the temperature a bit. I don't want him to get a chill.'

'No.' Thea's forefinger traced the baby's cheek lovingly, and Joe wondered bleakly what it must be like to give birth, to have something—no, someone—someone so indisputably your own—someone who needed you, who would love you without question and despite your flaws.

He felt suddenly, overwhelmingly alone, excluded, superfluous to Thea's happiness. 'I'll get you a cup of tea,' he muttered, and ran downstairs. He supposed she ought to go into hospital, just to be on the safe side. He filled the kettle and flicked on the outside light, surveying the garden. The wind was quieter now, the trees moving less. It would be safe now.

The phone was still out, but he had the mobile. Perhaps he'd call an ambulance and have them both taken to hospital, just to be sure.

He took her up the tea and told her what he had done, and she smiled benignly, as if she were on another planet. 'Thanks, Joe,' she said. He'd expected an argument, and was a bit surprised.

However, he wasn't about to provoke one by putting thoughts into her head! Instead he gathered together her things, and some for the baby, and within minutes an ambulance arrived and Thea and the baby were loaded and driven away.

He followed in the car, went up to his ward and explained that she should be admitted under William Parry. Then, having made sure she was comfortable and in safe hands, he came home, cleared up the devastation in her bedroom and went down to the sitting room.

What the hell, he thought. He poured himself a hefty Scotch, sat down in the chair Thea seemed to favour and stared blankly out of the window. Sylvester came and made himself at home, kneading Joe's leg with his claws and dribbling disgustingly with ecstasy, but Joe couldn't chuck him off.

Not tonight, when he felt so alone anyway.

'She had a little boy, old son. And it's Valentine's

Day today. I even bought her a box of chocolates.' He gave a short huff of laughter. 'She gave me heart failure and someone else's baby.'

Had he been the father it would, of course, have been the most wonderful Valentine's Day gift. He wondered if she was thinking about Mike now and, if so, how she could bear the sadness that he would never see his little son.

The Scotch blurred in the glass, and Joe blinked hard. Damn. Whatever was wrong with him? He was used to babies. He delivered them every day. This one was no different.

But he knew it was, and always would be, because it was Thea's, and Thea would always have a very special place in his heart. . :

Thea lay in the little single room at the side of the ward and listened to the quiet bustle. It was the middle of the night, and she had been seen and checked by a young doctor who had clerked her—checked her and made a set of notes on her admission—and declared that she had had a trauma-free delivery and would need no sutures, for which Thea was heartily grateful. It felt bad enough as it was!

Her eyes strayed yet again to the cot at the side of the bed. What an incredible, perfect little being he was. Thea smiled tiredly and watched her baby sleep. Someone else's was screaming blue murder down the corridor. They seemed to get so frightfully angry, she thought fondly. It must be terribly frustrating not to have the gift of speech.

But for now her baby at least was peaceful, and Thea

lay there watching him and thinking about her relief when she had seen the sweep of Joe's headlights in the window. If he hadn't come back when he had, she wasn't sure if she could have coped alone.

She wondered how she would feel seeing him in the cold light of morning, after their brother/sister relationship had taken such a biological shift with her delivery. Embarrassed, probably, she decided, but nothing could take away her gratitude, and she had been so pleased to have him there with her she wouldn't have cared if she'd been in Piccadilly in broad daylight!

A nurse came in and smiled at her. 'All right?' she asked.

'Fine. I was just looking at him.'

The nurse came closer and peered into the cot. 'He's lovely. Funny, it's been all girls this week, and now tonight we've got three boys already.'

'Have you been busy?' Thea asked her.

She rolled her eyes. 'Have we! It must have been the storm—it's brought them all out! Still, fortunately nothing nasty or too complicated. You're Mr Armitage's sister, aren't you?'

Thea smiled. 'Sort of. He lived with my family when he was a teenager, after his parents died. He isn't really my brother, but nothing will stop him behaving like he is!'

The nurse chuckled. 'He does love to look after people. He mollycoddles all the mums—they all adore him. He's such a softy. Did he tell you he nearly lost a baby today?'

Thea shook her head. 'No—there wasn't really time. Tiddly-winks there was making his appearance in a bit of a hurry. What happened?'

'Nasty presentation. He was brilliant, really saved the day, and the look on his face when the baby was delivered and yelled—wow! You would have thought it was his. I mean, we all get involved, but I think if that baby had died a part of him would have died too. We know it happens, but somehow he takes it harder. Some of the doctors cope well with the tragedies we get here, but him—he really seems to take it to heart. He goes very quiet and seems to withdraw into himself—as if he takes it personally. You'd think it was his fault.'

'Maybe he thinks it is.'

The nurse shrugged. 'Who knows? He's not that approachable otherwise, so I don't suppose I'll ever get round to asking! Do you fancy a hot drink, while you're awake?'

Thea did, and a few minutes later the nurse came back with a cup. 'Horlicks,' she said. 'Might help you sleep. There's a funny high you go through just after having a baby, and sometimes you just have to lie awake and let it all sink in. If you don't sleep, don't worry. You will tomorrow.'

She didn't—at least, not much. Instead she lay there and stared at her baby, and wondered what Mike would have thought of him, and decided he would have been absolutely smitten. What a tragedy that he hadn't had the chance to see him, or even to know that he existed.

'He would have been proud of you, little one,' she whispered. 'Very proud.'

As Joe walked into the maternity unit he wondered how Thea was feeling. How would she react to seeing him this morning? Would she be embarrassed? Maybe. He

wasn't. It had been too great a privilege to deliver her
baby for other, less important feelings to get in the way.

He ran up the stairs two at a time, the only exercise
he had time for in his busy schedule. He had picked
up a bunch of flowers from the garage opposite—early
daffodils to cheer her up and bring the spring inside. Last
night's chocolates were clutched in his hand together
with the flowers, and he found himself hurrying down
the corridor towards her room.

'Morning, Mr Armitage! You're in bright and
early today!'

He threw a grin over his shoulder. 'Morning, Staff.
I've come to see Dr Stow—how is she?'

'Fine. She didn't sleep much. I think she was too busy
looking at the baby. She's feeding him now—go on in.'

Damn. He didn't want to just walk into her room
without her consent while she was breast-feeding in case
she found his presence an embarrassment. Last night had
been unavoidable. Now she had her dignity back and her
pride to think about. He knocked.

'Come in,' she sang, sounding cheerful and quite
unbothered.

'It's Joe,' he warned her.

'Well, come in, then! Come and see your little almost-
nephew!'

He went in, and found to his relief that she had finished
the feed and was sitting up in bed with the baby against
her shoulder.

'We're learning how to burp,' she told him with a
grin. 'So far he's not wildly good at it, and neither am I!'

He chuckled, and, perching on the edge of the bed, he
dropped a kiss on her cheek, brushed the baby's fine,

downy hair with a fingertip and held out the flowers and chocolates.

'Here. I got the flowers this morning, but the chocs were for last night. Under the circumstances I forgot to give them to you.'

She took the flowers in her free hand and buried her nose in them. 'Mmm. Woods and leaf-mould and fresh spring mornings. Thank you, Joe. And truffles—heavens. Trying to help me get my figure back?' she teased.

He grinned awkwardly. 'They were just a silly impulse. I was getting petrol and I saw a banner saying it was Valentine's Day. I remembered my first February with you, when you made me a card at school and I had to pretend not to know it was from you. I thought it was time to return the favour.'

She laughed and held out her arm to him, drawing him down to give him a quick hug. As he straightened he cupped the baby's head with his hand and it felt warm and soft and wonderful.

The lump reappeared in his throat, and he cleared it self-consciously.

'So, Mr Baby-doctor, what do you think of your almost-nephew?' Thea asked him.

'What do I think?' He cleared his throat again. 'I think I need a better look, and you aren't making much progress with this burping nonsense. Perhaps an expert should have a go.'

She handed the baby over a little clumsily, obviously terrified in case she dropped him or didn't support his head right. Joe always found it amusing that new mothers took such care. After the babies had survived the rigours of delivery he was sure a little casual handling wouldn't make a great deal of difference. However, out of respect for her feelings he took, great care, although he could happily have held the little infant with one of his big hands.

He turned him against his shoulder, rubbed one hand up his back and the child let loose a burp that a lager lout would have been proud of.

Thea's eyes widened. 'Good heavens, baby, whatever was that?'

'That was eating too much too fast. He's clearly a little piglet. What are you going to call him?'

'Michael, I thought. Michael Joseph, after his father and you. Does he look like a Michael?'

Joe, unbelievably touched at having the baby named after him, held him away from his shoulder and squinted at him to cover his emotions. 'Do you look like a Michael?' he asked the little boy gruffly. 'Yeah, maybe. Your nose is squiffy, little one.'

Thea jackknifed up in bed. 'Where?'

Joe grinned. 'It'll straighten. They often get a bit squashed in the process. Don't worry.'

She leant back against the pillows. 'Are you sure?'

'Quite certain—aren't I, Michael? You're beautiful, squiffy nose and all, aren't you, my little friend?'

Michael blew a milky bubble at Joe and fixed him with serious deep blue eyes. Already they were tinged with brown. They'd be like Thea's, Joe thought, melting dark brown eyes, totally irresistible. He could hear it now. 'Uncle Joe, can I have a Ferrari?' 'Sure, Mike— what colour?' Sucker. He dropped a kiss on the downy head and handed him back to his mother before he made a fool of himself.

'Can you put him in his cot?' Thea asked. 'I'm dying for a glass of water and I don't trust myself not to pour it all over him.'

He laid him down on his side and tucked the covers round him, feeling altogether too much for an almost-uncle. What the hell would he be like if he were a real uncle—or even a real father?

The idea almost took his breath away.

CHAPTER THREE

WILLIAM PARRY came to see Thea later that morning. He was tall, dark, drop-dead gorgeous and had a delightful bedside manner. He admired the baby, looked at Thea's notes, asked how she was feeling, checked her over thoroughly but briefly and declared her fit as a flea.

'You're quite obviously designed for motherhood,' he said with a grin. 'You can go home whenever you're feeling strong enough, but if there's nobody to look after you perhaps it would be an idea to stay in as long as possible and have a rest.'

Thea smiled wanly. 'Gosh, that sounds tempting,' she murmured. 'I must confess to being a bit tired.'

His grin was gone, replaced by genuine concern. 'You don't want to overdo it and get exhausted, and Joe said you were pretty wiped out when you arrived. If you find you can rest in here, perhaps it would be as well to stay for five days or so.'

'If they don't mind having me,' Thea said with a rueful smile. 'I'll probably start interfering and getting in the way. You know what it's like—once a doctor and all that. I'll be out there poking my nose into the notes and eavesdropping on conversations just to stay sane!'

William laughed. 'I'm sure they won't mind. Have you done any obstetrics?'

She shook her head. 'Not yet. It would have been my next rotation, but my husband died and I found out I was pregnant, and frankly it was such a ghastly year there wasn't time for anything else.'

'No, I'm sure.' His face lost all its sparkle for a moment. 'My first wife died when she was very pregnant. I found it very hard to motivate myself then. Life just didn't seem to be worth bothering with.'

Thea opened her mouth to commiserate, but couldn't find any words. Instead she just shook her head mutely and gave him an understanding smile. And she did understand. Even though she'd known it was coming, Mike's death had hit her hard. How much worse to have been in William's position and lost a baby as well. She wondered how his wife had died. She'd have to ask Joe.

'So,' he said, visibly shaking off the memory and returning to their original subject, 'you'll stay in for a while?'

'I'll give it a whirl. I expect all your colleagues will come to you on Monday morning and beg you to discharge me!'

He laughed. 'I doubt it. You'll brighten the place up a bit. Anyway, Joe's on take this weekend so he'll be in and out. I expect he'll keep you in order.'

'Hmm. No doubt he'll try. Old habits die hard.'

He left, still chuckling, and promised to look in on Monday and make sure she'd been behaving.

She meant to. She really did, but the bustle and industry were too much for her, and, slipping out of bed, she went up to the nurses' station.

The ward sister looked up and smiled at her. 'Hello, Dr Stow. Can I get you something?'

'Not really. I was just going for a wander. It's a bit quiet in the side-ward.'

'That was Joe's idea—he thought you'd be able to rest better. Do you want to come out into a larger ward? I've got a four-bedder with space.'

Thea shook her head. 'No, it's OK. I'll sleep better at night, so long as you don't mind if I come out to socialise a little!'

The sister laughed. 'Good heavens, no. Do what you want. How's the feeding going?'

'Fine. I learnt how to burp him—I hand him to Joe.'

They both laughed, and then Thea gave a rueful sigh. 'I think I've got withdrawal from medicine, actually. I find what you're all doing out here much more interesting than the magazines I found to look at.'

'Are you going back to work?'

'I will do.' Thea shrugged slightly. 'I'll have to, anyway, to support us both, but I think I'd want to fairly soon even without a financial need. Part-time, anyway. I've almost finished my GP rotations, and I'd like to have a go at obstetrics. I wasn't really interested before, but now it fascinates me. I suppose it's because I've read a lot more about it recently.'

'Nothing like a bit of personal experience to bring things to life. I wouldn't have worked in maternity for love nor money until I'd had my children. Then it seemed perfectly natural!' The sister stood up. 'We're quiet now. Why don't you come round the ward with me and have a look at it? It's quite interesting, and of course you missed all the delivery room and things like that by opting out.'

Thea laughed. 'It was hardly deliberate, believe me! I know having a baby at home by candlelight on

Valentine's Day sounds frightfully romantic, but trust me, I was terrified!'

'Even with Joe there? He's always so calming.'

Thea chuckled. 'I don't think he felt very calm—especially when I insisted on getting up and walking round in the second stage!'

'No, I can imagine that! Right, let's go and have a snoop round the ward. My name's Jenny, by the way. Can I call you Thea?'

'Of course.'

They shared a smile, and for the first time since she had arrived in Suffolk Thea began to feel she might be not only safe but happy. Jenny was easy to talk to, very friendly and seemed to take Thea at face value. There were no insincere commiserations about the loss of her husband, no inquisitive remarks about her relationship with Joe—just one professional woman talking to another.

It was the first time in ages she had been treated in that way, and it felt wonderful.

They toured the ward, starting with the day room and kitchen, the sluices, past the wards full of happy mums and mostly happy babies, down to the delivery suites with a wide variety of birth options.

'You've got birthing pools,' Thea said in surprise.

'Yes, although women mostly use them now just for the labour. They were in constant demand a few years ago, but now they're not used as much, although they can help to relax and speed things up. We've got all sorts of options, actually—chairs, mats on the floor, things to kneel on and hang from. Really, whatever people want to do when they're in labour, we try and accommodate it, but we still have beds for the people who just want to lie down, and of course we've got properly equipped delivery rooms with all the relevant emergency equipment in case things go wrong, but it doesn't often happen. Mostly it's straightforward.'

'So if I'd got here in time I could have walked round? Rats.'

They both laughed, then Jenny said, 'You ought to try and do your obstetrics rotation here. We've got a vacancy coming up in a couple of months, I believe—why don't you ask Joe?'

'Because he'll say I should be at home with the baby.'

'Would he? I wouldn't have thought he'd be so dogmatic.'

Thea shrugged. 'Maybe. I don't really know him as well as I used to. Perhaps he's changed. Anyway, there would be all sorts of problems, I'm sure. He might not want me working in the same department.'

Jenny's brows twitched together in a little frown. 'But it would be so convenient. There's a crèche in the hospital now, too, you know. Lots of people go back to work with really quite young babies, and they seem to get on all right. You could always ask him.'

Thea smiled slightly. 'Perhaps I will. Anyway, I need to get through the first few weeks before I worry about work. I may fall apart with the interrupted nights.'

Jenny chuckled. 'No way. You're a doctor. You'll catnap and be fine. It's people who've never had to wake in the night that find they can't cope. You won't have a problem. None of the doctors do, and we've had dozens, God knows. We have a fairly young staff on the whole and lots of their families have been born in these wards. It's quite fun.'

They went back up the ward then, Jenny to deal with a patient, Thea to return to her room and think over the other woman's words. Would she like to return to work? And if so, here? With Joe?

Would he want her underfoot at work as well as at home? It was rather a lot to demand of a friendship that had survived the years on very little contact. Perhaps it would make things very awkward if she asked him. She'd have to start making subtle noises, but not yet. She'd give him a day or two to get used to her presence and give them both a chance to see how they got on with the baby around to complicate their relationship.

If anything, she discovered a little while later, the baby seemed to enhance it, because Joe was obviously a marshmallow where infants were concerned. She heard his firm stride coming, then a knock, and at her call he stuck his head round the door and winked at her with one lazy grey-blue eye. 'Hi. How's Mum?'

She smiled. 'Fine. As the saying goes, mother and baby both doing well. How's the surrogate uncle?'

The surrogate uncle in question was peering into the baby's cot and stroking the baby's cheek with a distracted expression on his face. At Thea's words he lifted his head and grimaced. 'Busy. I've come in to do an elective Caesarean section with attitude—she's gone into labour early.'

'How frightfully inconvenient of her.'

'Isn't it?'

They shared a smile. 'Things OK?' he asked her. 'You finding your way around all right?'

'Uh-huh. They're all very helpful. It's fun. You've got a nice staff.'

He grinned. 'Yes, we have. We're very lucky.' He glanced at his watch and sighed. 'Oh, well, I suppose I'd better go and do it and leave Michael to sleep.'

'Yes, don't wake him up; he's only just gone off. Pop in later and have a cuddle after you've done your op.'

'I will. I feel I've hardly seen him yet, and that will never do.' He saluted, winked again and left, and Thea stared after him, wondering why it was that the room felt suddenly so empty without him. . .

Joe tried to concentrate, but it was difficult. The patient had been given her epidural anaesthetic, and she and her husband were waiting for him to produce their new baby like a magician with a rabbit.

He stroked the scalpel over the skin and watched the thin stream of blood well in the incision line. He didn't see it, though. What he saw was Thea, her face pale but more rested now, the baby beside her sleeping peacefully, both of them fine thanks to his timely arrival home the night before. And what if he had been delayed still further, or unable to get home because of fallen trees? It had been a hell of a storm, and the wind had still been gusting.

What if he'd failed them?

Unseen by him, the scrub nurse swabbed and sucked, then cleared her throat pointedly. He started, focused on the incision and the scalpel lying useless in his hand. What the hell was the matter with him, daydreaming like this? Never mind Thea, he was failing this mother, here and now! He stroked again, then again, and they were through the abdominal wall.

The uterus was there, squirming slightly with the young life it contained, and Joe quickly and carefully opened the wall with a small lateral incision in the lower segment, opened the membranes and eased the baby out, then held it up for the proud parents to see.

'You've got a son,' he told them with a smile, and the midwife clamped the cord, cut it and, wrapping the now screaming baby in a towel, lifted him over the drapes and laid him in his father's arms.

Joe and the scrub nurse concentrated on tidying up the carnage and closing, and yet again Joe found his mind wandering back to Thea and her baby. What would she have done if she hadn't managed to find him? Where would she be living? Who would look after her?

And where would she go when she left him?

His mouth hardened. Nowhere. She'd stay near him if not with him, so he could continue to keep an eye on her and young Michael Joseph. He'd be damned if he'd let her drop out of sight again the way she had for the past three years. The girl needed a keeper, clearly, and who better than him?

Yes. He'd look after her. Someone had to.

Of course she might meet another man and fall in love again, but that could be years away. Still, she was a beautiful woman now. It could be any time—

'Not yet,' he muttered.

'What?'

He looked up into the puzzled eyes of the scrub nurse. 'Sorry. Miles away.'

He sutured with care, layer by layer, and at last he

was finished. He checked the woman's condition with the anaesthetist, congratulated the parents on their lovely baby and strode out of the operation room, opening the door with one firm thrust of his big shoulder, stripping off gloves and hat and mask as he went, lobbing his gown into the bin as he passed it.

He could feel sweat trickling down between his shoulderblades, and he went into the changing room, stripped and turned on the shower. It was cold for a moment, taking his breath away, and then the hot came through and he stood under the pelting blast, water streaming over his hair and face and down over his restless body.

He felt irritated all of a sudden, in a hurry to get back to Thea. For the first time in his life his job hadn't absorbed him to the exclusion of all else, and he found it unsettling and confusing. Perhaps it was the storm, stirring up emotions and playing hell with his nerve-endings. Or maybe it was due to Thea's arrival and the wash of guilt he felt at the fact that she had suffered all through this last year and he hadn't known about it.

Still, that was as much her fault as his. He'd lost touch with her shortly after her father died. They'd both moved, both home and job. Even so she'd managed to find him. He could just as easily have found her.

His conscience plagued him now that he hadn't made the effort, but it had been deliberate, in a way.

He'd made the offer to help, and it had been time to stand back and let her find her feet. There came a time in everybody's life when help became a hindrance. You had to find yourself, and that was hard when you were busy being the person your loved ones expected you to be.

God knows, he'd changed enough. He thought back to the difficult, sulky boy he'd been at fifteen, with no drive, no confidence, just a seething mass of insecurity and misunderstanding. It was thanks to Thea and her parents that he was alive, but it was little short of a miracle that he'd found his niche and was now making a success of his life. Workwise, anyhow, in the career his own father had followed until his untimely death.

Emotionally, though, he was very wary. There was no one he was close to, no one to warm the dark nights when the loneliness crept up on him, but it was by choice. It was some time now since his last relationship had foundered on the rocks of his caution. Perhaps he just wasn't cut out for romance.

For some inexplicable reason an image of Thea leapt into his mind, her head resting back against a pillow, her eyes soft and tender in the candlelight. She looked so vulnerable, as she had just after Michael's birth. What if he hadn't been there?

He pulled himself up abruptly. He had been there, and any further speculation would achieve nothing. He'd just have to make sure he was there in the future, because one thing he knew for sure—if anything happened to either of them now, his guilt would be a cross he'd bear for the rest of his damnable and wretched life.

On the other hand he didn't want to crowd her. That might drive her away, stubborn, independent little thing that she was, and then God alone knows what trouble she'd get herself into. Sighing with frustration, he flicked off the water and stood for a moment, head propped against the cool tiles, wondering how the hell he was going to keep her safe from herself. He just had this nasty feeling. . .

Still troubled, he scrubbed his body viciously with a towel and pulled on his clothes again. He had promised to go back and visit her, but he needed space to think. Instead he checked on his patient, sent a message to Thea via the ward staff that he had been called out, and went home, pulled on his old work-clothes and set about sawing a gap through the pine tree that blocked his drive.

The wind was still gusting but he didn't care. Perhaps it would blow away the cobwebs and clear his mind of the image of Thea lying in bed, her hair spread out on the pillow, her wide, innocent eyes lifeless because he had been delayed and let her down the final, vital time. . .

Joe didn't come back again. Thea received a message to say he was too busy, and she was stunned at the disappointment she felt by his failure to keep his word. Joe always kept his word. Still, she told herself, he had sent her a message. It wasn't as if he just hadn't turned up. Anyway, he had probably made plans for today ages ago. After all, he had a life to lead—a life he'd been leading before her arrival on the scene.

Her common sense and natural fairness warred with her disappointment, and, pragmatist that she was, resignation came quickly. Anyway, she was busy with little Michael, and when the baby slept she found herself drifting towards the nurses' station and the hub of activity.

She met one of the senior midwives, Bev Linari, and chatted happily to her about the cases she was dealing with. There were two women in labour that afternoon, and one was not doing too well.

'I may have to call Joe in,' Bev said in disappointment. 'I hate it when things go wrong and we have to resort to technology, but I think in this instance it's going to be inevitable. Still, we'll give her another hour or so and see if we can't wring some progress out of her.'

Bev went off to chivvy her patient, and Thea turned back to her room to see a huge hulk of a man dressed in old cords and a white coat bending over Michael's cot. It was a doctor's coat, but the cords didn't go with it, and alarm bells started screaming in Thea's head.

She ran back to the little room and grabbed him by the arm, oblivious to his vast bulk compared with her tiny frame. 'What are you doing to him?' she demanded furiously. 'Leave him alone!'

The man straightened, his body unyielding under her frantic tugging, and laid a huge hand over her fists clenched in his sleeve. 'Shh, easy! It's all right—I'm a paediatrician—a children's doctor.'

She met his eyes, the colour of warm toffee, infinitely kind, and the fury drained out of her. Chastened, she slumped on the bed. 'Sorry,' she said numbly. 'It was the trousers that did it. You don't look like a doctor. I thought. . .'

'That I was going to hurt your baby. I'm sorry I worried you—I came straight out of the garden in answer to an urgent call. The name's Andrew Barrett, and you must be Thea Stow, Joe's friend.' He held out a hand, and her own was swallowed in it and squeezed reassuringly. 'Jenny asked me to do a paediatric check as I was on the ward.'

Immediately alarm bells rang again, but this time for

a quite different reason. Thea's eyes widened in horror.
'Why? What's wrong with him?'

'Nothing, as far as I'm aware. It's just routine.'

'Oh.' She swallowed her fear and looked at Michael,
sleeping in his little transparent plastic cot, oblivious to
the scene that had been played out around him.
'I'm sorry.'

'No, I'm sorry. I should have come and found you—
I was just having a little peek first. I'm going to have to
wake him, I'm afraid.'

Thea flapped a hand. 'Go ahead. Do whatever you
have to do.'

He was gentle but thorough. First he looked at him,
examining him to make sure that all was as it should be
and that there was nothing missing or out of place. He
turned him over, resting him on his hand while he
checked his spine with big, blunt fingers, then turned
him back and checked his limbs.

He noticed, as Thea had, the tiny flaw—the last two
toes of his right foot that were webbed together. 'Does
this worry you?' he asked. 'It can be operated on if
it does.'

She shook her head. 'His father was the same. It never
worried him.'

Andrew Barrett nodded, then went on with his examination. He tested his reflexes, checked his heart and eyes,
checked his hearing by clicking his fingers beside each
ear in turn and then apologised to him softly before taking
his tiny legs in his huge hands and checking his hips for
congenital dislocation.

He cried, as Andrew had, of course, known he would,
and he quickly refastened the nappy and lifted him to

his chest, soothing him with a murmur. Michael settled immediately, and Thea almost laughed aloud at herself for ever thinking this man could be a threat.

He turned to her with a smile. 'He's fine. None the worse for his precipitate arrival. How are you?'

'Fine. Delighted with him. I'm sorry I attacked you.'

He chuckled and laid the baby back in the cot. 'I'm just glad you don't weigh fifteen stone or I might not have come off so lightly,' he said with an infectious grin, and tucked the covers around the baby with gentle hands. 'If you're lucky he might go off to sleep again.'

He did, his tiny rosebud mouth soft and moist, his eyes twin creases in his face—quite unharmed by his ordeal. Laughing at herself for being so silly, Thea went to tell Jenny what she had done.

They had a good hoot over her assault on Andrew Barrett, and then, in a lull during the visiting period, she went into Jenny's office for tea. They had almost finished when a staff nurse came and tapped on the door.

'Mrs Breckwell's leaving in a few minutes,' she said to Jenny, and then turned to Thea. 'Your little one's yelling too.'

Thea groaned. 'I thought it was too good to be true that he'd drifted off again. Oh, well.' With a grin to Jenny, she made her way back to her room and picked the purple and furious baby out of the cot.

'Hush, little one, hush,' she soothed, and, settling herself on the bed, she unfastened her nightdress and latched the baby onto her nipple. He seemed strangely reluctant, Thea thought, and soothed his hair. Odd how the shape of his head had changed so much in twenty-four hours. It seemed rounder; the bones sliding over each other to take their proper place now that the business of delivery was completed, she supposed.

The baby fussed at her breast, and with a sigh she put him down in the cot to change his nappy. As she did so, a strange feeling came over her—a feeling of wrongness, of something not quite as it should be. The fear she had felt when she'd found Andrew Barrett bending over him returned, prickling at the edges of her sanity. Crazy. She was going crazy. Her baby was fine.

She looked at him, and thought again how his features had altered. The squiffy nose was now straight too, but there was more than that—something more fundamental. She shook her head. No. She was imagining it.

She unfastened the nappy and pulled it away, and then stopped in confusion. She hadn't been wrong at all. The baby in Michael's cot wasn't Michael at all—it was a girl, someone else's child! Thea sat down on the bed with a plonk. So where was Michael, and how could they have got mixed up? He shouldn't even have been out of the room, so his cot couldn't have been muddled.

She looked at the label on the end of the cot, and no, it was definitely Michael's cot. How strange. Trying not to panic, she looked at the wristband and ankle band, and terror gripped her like a vice. The bands were Michael's, but the baby wasn't hers.

Someone had stolen her baby!

CHAPTER FOUR

THEA had never known a fear like the one that racked her now. Yanking open the door to her room, she ran out into the ward. Jenny was at the nurse's station and Thea seized her arm.

'Michael's gone,' she said urgently. 'Someone's swapped the identity bands and taken him—the baby in his cot is a girl!'

Jenny's eyes widened, and, leaping to her feet, she hurried after Thea and looked stunned at the half-naked baby girl in the cot. Like Thea, she checked the little plastic bracelets on wrist and ankle, noted the stretched straps, which showed they had been taken off to swap them, and quickly covered the baby again.

'My God,' she muttered, and then ran back to the nurses' station and snatched up the phone, jabbing at numbers. 'Reception? Don't let anyone leave the building, please. A baby's been switched. No one—no, not even with a nurse. Oh, Lord—stop her, please. Get Security to escort her back up.' She looked up at Thea. 'Mrs Breckwell was just leaving. They'll bring her back up. She had a girl—her fifth. It must be her.'

As Jenny turned to snap instructions to the shocked nurses hovering nearby, Thea began to shake helplessly. What if the woman downstairs was too slow? What if Mrs Breckwell had already left the building with Michael? Would she ever see him again?

'Please, God, no,' she whispered. 'No. . .'

Joe, preoccupied with his thoughts, shouldered aside the door and almost collided with the receptionist as she ran towards him.

'Oh, Mr Armitage, help me—stop that woman from leaving, please! There's been a baby snatch—'

Joe spun on his heel, shoved the door aside again and sprinted to the kerb just as the taxi door was closing on the woman inside.

He yanked the door open, instructed the taxi driver to wait and leant over, one hand on the door, the other on the roof of the car. The couple inside stared at him, the man belligerently, the woman with something like fear hovering in the back of her eyes.

He addressed the woman. 'I'm sorry to have to ask you this, but I wonder if you'd mind coming back inside for a moment so we can clear up a little problem?'

'What problem?' the man snarled. 'We're late as it is.'

'I'm sorry, but it really is most important that you come with me,' Joe said, implacable. He addressed the woman again, his mind focused on one thing and one only. If he could only persuade her. . .

'Let me hold the baby so you can get out more easily,' he suggested, praying she would fall for it, but the man was too quick.

'Don't do it, Carol. You stay right where you are—the baby too. We have to go—'

Joe cut the man off. 'I'm sorry, I'm afraid I really must insist.'

He held out his hands towards the little bundle, but the woman holding the baby didn't move. Then, without warning, tears welled in her terrified eyes. 'It was Stan's idea—'

'Shut up, you stupid woman! What the hell are you saying?'

She turned to her husband. 'I'm telling the truth,' she said unevenly. 'I'm sick of saying what you tell me to say about everything, and this has gone too far.' She turned back to Joe, ignoring the blustering man beside her. 'He said we had to do it. He wanted a boy. It was all he ever wanted, and I've only ever been able to give him girls—' She broke off, her pain choking off the words, and with trembling hands she lifted the baby and placed it carefully in Joe's waiting hands.

'Here—take him back to his poor mother. I never wanted him anyway. I only ever wanted my little girl. . .'

Joe carefully cradled the baby up against his chest and backed out of the car, to find two uniformed security guards waiting to escort the couple back into the building. One of them stopped Stan Breckwell's bolt from the car, and, gripping him securely with one arm behind his back, frogmarched him into the hospital.

They took the lift, Joe and the baby on one side, the security guards and the baby-snatchers on the other, and as the doors opened Thea was there waiting.

'Is it Michael?' she asked calmly, but he saw her eyes were filled with fear.

Startled, Joe looked for the first time at the baby in his arms. The little nose was a bit crooked, the eyes staring up at him so solemnly were navy blue tinged with brown. Just to be sure he tugged off the right sock, and there were the toes, webbed like his father's. A convulsive rage gripped Joe. 'Yes, Tink, it's Michael,' he said softly, and with enormous care he placed the baby back in her waiting arms.

Then, grim-lipped and silent, he followed the entourage back into the ward to find out what the hell had been going on.

'So that's it,' Joe explained to her. 'The husband wanted a son to take over the farm, the wife is too weak to refuse him anything, even something as major as this, and so he told her to switch the baby for a boy just before they left. I think they really imagined they'd get away with it, too!'

Thea, still shocked and badly shaken, held Michael up against her shoulder and nuzzled her cheek against his downy head, still unable to believe he was back in her arms unharmed. The police had been wonderful, but all she wanted was to crawl away and hide. 'I thought it was funny when his nose was straight,' she said unsteadily, and then suddenly and without warning a great sob ripped through her and huge, heavy tears cascaded down her cheeks.

Joe gathered Thea against his shoulder, the baby between them, and, cradling her head against the side of his face, he held her, one hand cupping her nape, the other round her back supporting her hard against him. 'Easy, sweetheart,' he murmured. 'Easy now. He's all right. It's all over.'

But the great ripping sobs continued to tear through her, and Joe just held her and soothed her and let her cry. After a while she quietened, but she still wasn't ready to leave the safety of Joe's arms. He was so strong, so powerful, and she felt so secure. As secure as she could here, in this place where Michael had been taken from her. 'I want to go home,' she said when she could speak.

'I thought you might,' he murmured. 'Jenny's just seeing to your discharge papers. I'm taking you home just as soon as I've delivered this baby Bev's having problems with.'

Just then there was a tap at the door. 'Forget it,' Bev said. 'You were too slow; we've managed without you.'

Her grin denied any great problem, and Thea felt herself relax a little 'Does that mean we can go home now?' she asked him softly.

'Yes, Tink, it does. Put your dressing gown on and we'll be out of here in a minute. I'll get a wheelchair.'

He was back in a moment, together with Jenny, who gave Thea a hug and kissed her cheek. 'OK?' she asked in concern.

'I will be.'

'I'm so sorry it had to happen,' Jenny said with real remorse in her voice. 'I could kick myself for not being more alert, for not anticipating it.'

'It wasn't your fault,' Thea tried to reassure her, but Jenny shook her head.

'I'm the ward sister. The buck stops here, remember? But it's never happened before, and if I have anything to say about it it will never happen again. We're going to have an inquiry into our working practices, I hope, to make sure it isn't possible for anyone else to try, but in the meantime I hope it won't put you off coming back to work here.'

Thea caught Joe's puzzled glance and remembered that she hadn't told him about her conversation with Jenny.

Heavens, had it really been only that morning?

'I'll see,' she promised vaguely, and then, turning to Joe, she looked up at him with desperation in her eyes. 'Can we go now?' she asked quietly.

'Sure.' He sat her in the wheelchair, Michael clamped firmly in her arms, and as they reached Joe's car and Thea was helped into the back with the baby on her knee some of the paralysing fear began to leave her. 'Put your seat belt on,' Joe instructed, and lifted the baby away until she had. Then he settled the little bundle back into her empty arms and slid behind the wheel, leaving her to stare down at the beloved face of her child all the way home.

By the time Joe turned into the drive and edged his way between the sawn ends of the pine tree that still spanned the front garden, the baby's features were etched on her mind for ever. She could have found him in a crowd of thousands.

Hopefully she would never have to. . .

'So what did Jenny mean?'

'Mean?'

'About you working in the hospital.'

'Oh.' Thea blinked a little. That conversation seemed so far away now. 'We were talking about whether I'd go back to work when Michael was a bit older, and I said I quite fancied obstetrics. It was nothing serious, really.'

Joe nodded thoughtfully, then continued to regard Thea in silence, his chin resting on steepled fingers. They were in the sitting room, Thea tucked up on the sofa with a blanket and the baby, Joe sprawling nearby, his elbows propped on the arms of the chair.

'Are you all right?' he asked softly.

She shrugged. Of course not. Someone had tried to steal her baby. 'I'll live,' she said without emotion.

'I know that. I just wondered if you would be able to deal with your anger.'

Her head jerked up, her eyes locking with his. 'How did you know I was angry?' she asked him, and then chided herself. Of course he knew. Joe always knew.

It was his turn to shrug. 'I would be. I am, and it isn't even my child. I think you'll find the investigation is very thorough, and security has already been stepped up. I'm amazed they managed to get so far.'

Thea wasn't amazed. She was appalled, and she couldn't imagine how she would have felt if her baby had actually left the hospital. It was enough that the other woman had touched him. The first thing she had done when they'd arrived home was bath him and dress him in his own new clothes to wash away the invisible stain left by all that had happened.

She wondered if the other woman would feel the same. If the babies had simply become muddled up, would it have felt so terrible? Thea thought probably not. She had expected to feel revulsion because she had breast-fed the other baby but, strangely enough, she didn't. It had been so tiny, so lovely, so innocent—there was nothing to feel revulsion about. The thing that struck her most was that the woman had actually left her own child behind in favour of another, regardless of sex.

Thea could no more have done that than fly, and in the midst of her anger she felt a sudden, enormous pity

for the woman who had been forced into such a terrible
act by her bully of a husband.

'Penny for them,' Joe said quietly.

Thea attempted a smile. She didn't feel she could put
her thoughts into words—not quite yet. They were still
so unformed. 'Just thinking about how she must feel
now. Will she get her baby back?'

Joe shrugged. 'That all depends. For now, the baby's
the subject of an emergency protection order, and social
services are investigating the family background. I
imagine the courts might send her to prison.'

'Him,' Thea corrected, but Joe shook his head.

'She swapped them.'

'But at what cost to herself? And why? Does he
beat her?'

'Probably. He's that sort. Taciturn, physically powerful, mentally a shade unhinged—yes, I expect he beats
her. They'll be looking at the children too, for evidence
of any abuse or harm.'

Thea shivered at his words. Her father had always
been so gentle, and Mike had been too, his hands on her
almost tentative. Joe had been gentle too, in her childhood, and now, still, he touched her with tenderness and
respect.

That was the missing ingredient, of course, in the
Breckwells' relationship. Respect. Respect for Mrs
Breckwell, for their four daughters, for their new baby
so easily discarded in favour of one of the 'right' sex—
Thea felt so sorry for them all.

She looked down at Michael on her lap and wondered
if she would feel any differently about him if he
were a girl.

No. Of course not. He was Mike's baby, his last gift to the world, and that would always be the most significant thing. His gender was immaterial. She brushed his cheek with her knuckles, marvelling at the softness of the delicate, peach-bloom skin. Thank God he was back with her. She choked back another wave of tears, closing her eyes against them and resting her head back against the cushions.

He was safe now; that was the only thing that mattered—

'You should be in bed.'

Joe's words cut across her thoughts, and she opened her eyes and found him watching her, his own eyes veiled by the shadows cast by the table lamp behind him.

'I am tired,' she confessed. 'Can't I just stay here for a while? Going upstairs seems so much effort.'

'I'll help you.'

And he did, quietly and without fuss supporting her up the stairs and into her room, running her a bath, taking Michael from her and changing his nappy before tucking him into the little crib beside her bed.

He laid out a clean nightdress for her, turned back the bed and went to make her a cup of tea while she bathed. He was back before she was finished, hovering nearby in case she got into difficulties, tucking her into bed with her tea and a host of promises about being nearby in the night.

He left the bathroom light on and the door ajar, and her own door he left open too, so he could hear her if she called him.

'Are you going back downstairs?' she asked, dreading being alone and yet unwilling to ask him to stay.

'No. Well, only to lock up and check the cat and set the alarm. Then I'm coming up to bed. I'll leave my door open so I can hear you.'

She lay there and listened, and, sure enough, within a couple of minutes he was upstairs again, his softly murmured 'Goodnight, Tink,' wrapping round her like a buffer against the real world.

Sure she would be awake all night, she slid down the bed, rested her head on the soft, sweet-smelling pillow and fell instantly asleep.

Joe was less lucky. He lay for hours staring at the ceiling, listening for any sound and wondering at the primitive feelings of anger and possessiveness that had overwhelmed him when he'd realised that Michael had been the subject of the baby-snatch. Anybody would think the child was his own. . .!

At two-thirty the baby awoke, fidgeting at first and then getting into a full-blown bellow by the time Thea forced her eyes open.

Joe was there already, helping her sit up before handing the baby to her.

She was blurred with sleep, her hands uncooperative, and the baby failed to latch on properly, his hungry little mouth squeezing her nipple in the wrong place and making her gasp.

She prised him off and tried again, then finally turned her eyes to Joe. 'I can't do it,' she said helplessly.

He gave a short sigh, then with one hand cupped behind Michael's head and the other lifting her swollen, blue-veined breast towards the baby, he brushed Michael's cheek with the nipple and then, as the baby turned, mouth opening, he pressed the little face against her breast and she felt the nipple sink deep into the baby's mouth and the rhythmic suckling started again, this time without pain.

'OK?' His voice was gruff, but she hardly noticed.

She nodded, her eyes fixed on her baby, unable to look away. Apparently satisfied that Michael was suckling well and Thea was comfortable, Joe went down to the kitchen, made her a cup of tea and brought it back up just in time to wind the baby and hand him back for part two.

This time she managed to latch the baby on herself, so Joe took himself off to the other side of the room, sat in the armchair and closed his eyes.

Thea wondered if he was embarrassed at having to help her with such an intimate task. She wasn't. Joe never embarrassed her; he was always so matter-of-fact and calm, but she had a feeling she might embarrass him at times. Now, though, she was simply keeping him up. She spoke softly, in case he had drifted off. 'You look tired—why don't you go back to bed?'

He grunted. 'I'm fine. Tell me when you're finished and I'll change his nappy again.'

'I can manage—'

'So can I, and I haven't just gone through labour. It's scarcely twenty-four hours since you had him, Thea, and it's hardly been an average day. You should be resting.'

'You have to go to work—'

'Not till Monday.'

'I thought you were on call?'

'I swapped,' he confessed. 'I thought you'd need me

around, so could you please concentrate on needing me so I don't feel such a fraud?'

The words were said softly, and Thea laughed under her breath. 'If you say so, big brother,' she murmured.

'I do.' He closed his eyes again, and she looked down at her baby. His mouth was slack now, the greedy suckling stopped at last, his tiny fist relaxed against the swell of her breast. She eased him away, pulled her nightdress closed and lifted him against her shoulder, patting him hopefully.

Useless. 'Uncle Joe?' she said softly.

His eyes flicked open.

'You're the wind expert. Want to have a go?'

With a wry grin he hoisted himself out of his chair and took the baby from her, propping him against his shoulder. 'Come on, then, little man, let's show her how it's done,' he murmured.

He walked across the room and back, his voice soft and soothing, his big hand slowly, patiently circling against Michael's spine, and then right on cue a shattering burp ruptured the silence.

'You're a lager lout, MJ,' Joe said affectionately, and Thea sank back against the pillows with a smile and watched through the doorway as Joe changed the baby's nappy with typical efficiency while she drank her tea.

Then he tucked Michael back in his cot, said, 'See you in a few hours, little man,' and bent over Thea and brushed his lips lightly over her forehead. 'Sleep tight, Tink.'

He was at the door before she stopped him.

'Joe?'

He looked back, a strange expression in his eyes. 'Yes?'

'Thank you.'

His eyes darkened but he said nothing, just nodded wordlessly and went quietly out, leaving Thea alone with the sleeping baby and her restless thoughts.

The police came at ten the next morning, kind and very understanding, very thorough, checking every detail, and after a necessarily long-winded interview with the same policeman she had met last night she checked her statement and signed it.

'What will happen now?' she asked.

'They'll appear before the magistrate, charged with an offence of kidnapping or abduction, and then at some time in the future it'll go to court and they'll be tried and sentenced.'

'And the children?'

'In the care of social services at the moment, although I don't know what will happen in the future. I imagine there'll be a recommendation for psychiatric referral for the mother at least, if not both.' The policeman stood up and shook her hand, then brushed his knuckles over Michael's cheek. 'Lovely little chap. He won't know anything about it, of course.'

Thea stood up and walked to the window, staring sightlessly down the garden. 'I feel violated,' she told him. 'It's almost like rape—as if he's been raped. Isn't that crazy?'

'No. It's what I'd expect,' the policeman told her. 'It's a normal and healthy reaction to a threat to your child.' He hesitated for a moment, then went on, 'There's a

victim support group I could put you in touch with, so
you could talk your feelings through with someone who
understands—someone outside your family who's quite
independent of authority, who's trained to help you deal
with the emotional backlash you're going to feel from
this. Would you like me to do that, or do you want to
think about it?'

Thea swallowed. 'Perhaps in a few days?'

'Sure, I'll be in touch, anyway.'

Thea watched him go, so kind and thoughtful, yet
perforce dredging up the hideous events of the previous
day. By the time Joe came back into the room she was
shaking.

'Ah, Tink,' he murmured gruffly, and drew her into
his arms.

'It brought it all back,' she said unevenly. 'I thought
I'd put it behind me. . .'

'Why don't you do as he suggested and get in touch
with the victim support people? They really do help.'

She eased away from him, not wanting to leave the
safety of his arms but feeling she should be able to stand
on her own two feet. 'I didn't think I'd need it,' she
confessed. 'I really thought I'd be all right.'

'And so you will, but perhaps not without a little help
from someone who understands. When things happen to
people you love, feelings aren't always rational. Sometimes you just need someone there to be angry at,
someone to shout at and rage about the unfairness. You
want to shout at me, feel free. It might help.'

She met his eyes then. 'You understand, don't you?
How I feel?'

The blue-grey seemed to deepen to the colour of a

rain-lashed sky. 'Yes, Tink,' he said softly, and his voice was gravelly with her pain. 'I understand.' His voice so quiet that she wasn't sure she'd heard him right, he added, 'More than you will ever know. . .'

The days passed. Michael, or MJ as he became affectionately known, grew steadily. The windy weather disappeared, the sun came out and the early daffodils and crocuses nodded their heads in the mild, spring-like air.

At first Thea hardly dared to let Michael out of her sight, and if he slept too quietly she would panic and run to check that he was still there.

He was, of course, always, and gradually the tension left her. The victim support group was a great help, and so was the policeman, who came to see her regularly to check that she was doing OK and to inform her of the progress of the case.

The children were in care, the mother was back in the community but the father was in prison awaiting trial, accused of a whole plethora of offences against his wife and daughters. It seemed likely that Carol Breckwell would get off due to the mitigating circumstances, but the father was going down for several years if the policeman had anything to do with it.

Thea just felt immensely sorry for all of them, but as the days turned to weeks and February became March so her own emotions settled down and she began to enjoy her baby.

So, to her surprise, did Joe. He never shirked on the messy chores, either. If he was in the house, as often as not it was he who changed the baby's nappy, or bathed him, or flung the endless washing in the machine and hung it out to dry.

'So domesticated—you're a real treasure,' Thea teased him one day as he was ironing his shirts. 'You'll make someone a lovely wife one day.'

He gave a quiet snort of laughter, but there was an instant of tension in him that no one else would have detected. Thea wondered where it had come from, and why. A broken relationship? She had thought at the beginning that he might have bought his house with a woman in mind. Had the woman changed her mind, bottled out?

'Who was she?' Thea asked without thinking, and then could have kicked herself.

Joe went absolutely still. 'She?' he said in a voice rough with tension.

'Whoever you bought the house for.'

He looked at her, his eyes searching but unrevealing, then after a moment he continued to iron the shirt. 'Nobody special. I thought for a while she was, but then I realised I was just nesting. It didn't seem a good enough reason.'

'When was it?'

'Two years ago—a few months after I bought the house. She's married now to someone else—pregnant, I think. Anyway, she's happier than she would have been with me.'

Thea laughed softly. 'He must be an incredible man if he's made her happier than you could.'

Joe scoffed, 'You're just saying that so I'll keep changing the nappies,' he teased, and she grinned.

'Too right. What other use could you have?'

There was a sudden, almost palpable tension between them, broken finally by Joe's lopsided grin. 'I'm a dab hand at the ironing,' he said, and Thea's breath eased out in a soft gust.

She could hardly breathe, could hardly look at him, because her words had brought an image to mind of Joe as a husband, doing all the things a husband might do with his wife, and she found that the idea had an almost shockingly powerful appeal.

But Joe? Good old Joe, her childhood friend and confidant, the guiding star of her difficult teenage years? Joe, who had never turned her away no matter how irritating she'd become? Joe, who had opened his home to her without question or reservation, taking her and her baby in and giving them anything they needed for their happiness—that Joe?

Yes. Dear God, yes.

She loved him. Not as a sister, not as a friend, but as a woman—a woman with needs and passions and longings.

There was only one small drawback—Joe saw her as his sister, and nothing else.

He was talking now, and she struggled to concentrate, banishing her unruly thoughts.

'Do what?' she asked him.

'Your obstetrics rotation. Jenny discussed it with you some time ago.'

'At the Audley Memorial?'

'Is that a problem? Because of the Breckwells and Michael?'

She shook her head. 'No. No, not at all. I've put all that behind me. Anyway, I've been back to see them all.'

'It's just that if you do want the job you really ought to let me have something in writing to offer my colleagues so we can bypass all the official nonsense and take you on.'

She stared at him. 'What about an interview?'

He laughed quietly. 'Thea, do you want the job?'

She thought of leaving Michael during the day, the extra work and worry it would cause, the difficulties she would have to juggle. Then she thought of Joe and the money she owed him, the debt she could never repay, the future she had to carve for herself and Michael.

'Yes, I want the job,' she said, and her voice was firm.

'Good. That's fine. You can start at the beginning of May.'

And that was that.

CHAPTER FIVE

'HERE you go.'

Joe flicked a sealed envelope across the kitchen table at Thea, and she picked it up and opened it, puzzled. 'What is it?' she asked, staring at the folded sheet she had withdrawn.

'Sorry, I thought you could read,' he said mildly.

She rolled her eyes at him, then unfolded and glanced down at the letter in her hand. 'It's from you—what is it, a notice of eviction?' She said it lightly, but there was a thread of seriousness in her voice which Joe picked up on, as she might have known he would.

'Tink!' he reproached her softly. 'You know you and MJ are welcome here for as long as you want to stay. There will never be an eviction order.'

'Never is a long, long time,' she reminded him.

'I know,' he said, and his voice was bleak. 'I remember when they told me I'd never see my parents again. Believe me, Tink, I know how long never is. I meant what I said.'

Her heart thumped. Did he really mean it, or was he just being kind again? What about if he found another woman to build a future with? How would that woman cope with having another family already installed in what would be her home? 'You shouldn't make promises you can't keep,' she said quietly.

'But I can,' he said, just as quietly.

Their eyes locked, and in his she saw not only the straightforward honesty that was Joe but also something else, some element of conflict, as if his actions arose from a sense of duty.

Paying back the debt, no matter what the cost? She couldn't let him do that. She looked away.

'I'm crowding you. We've been here nearly three months.'

'Not even two and a half.'

'Whatever. I feel we're going to outstay our welcome.'

He snorted softly and shook his head. 'I can't seem to make you understand, Tink—I'm enjoying having you here. I like you. I even like your noisy, squalling baby.'

That much she knew was true. Thea's expression softened, and she looked into the baby bouncer on the floor beside her. MJ was asleep—for now. It wouldn't last long; he was due for another feed soon. He was growing so like her. Even she could see it.

'Are you going to read that thing, then?'

She looked down at the letter in her hand, surprised to see it there. She had forgotten about it. Her eyes scanned the typescript.

'"Dear Dr Stow"—heavens, that's very formal, Joe.'

'It is formal. It has to be. It's offering you the job.'

'Really?' Her heart skittered, and she scanned the page faster. 'So it is. Wow. You swung it with your colleagues.'

He grinned. 'They're pretty amenable. I told them you needed occupying so we could have some decent conversation in the evenings that didn't start and end with Michael.'

Thea felt herself withdraw. Was she boring him? He'd

just told her he enjoyed having her there. Was that a lie, formed out of his damnable and exaggerated sense of duty? Oh, Lord, she was sick of being beholden. Surely his debt, if it existed, was discharged now? She would take the job, of course—she'd always intended to—and she'd talk shop and entertain with anecdotes, and then just as she'd finished her rotation she'd get out of his way and go and take a job as a trainee in a general practice somewhere miles away. . .

The thought depressed her unbearably.

The first of May came almost before she could believe it. She had been to see the crèche and met the woman who ran it, and had taken to her at once. Her name was Angela, and she was a trained nursery nurse with years of experience and children of her own.

She was sensible and capable, had a good, reliable, hand-picked staff and she inspired confidence. The nursery was bright and colourful, full of stimulating things for the children to do and play with, and there was a quiet, subdued area for rest where the children could lie down and sleep if they were tired. On top of that, security was excellent.

She gave Michael a serious talking-to the day she started work.

'Now listen here,' she told him, 'Mummy's got to go and finish her training so she can look after you properly in the future, so you've got to be a good boy and have a lovely time with Angela and not be a worry, OK?'

'Why are you talking about yourself as if you're someone else?'

She whirled round, hand clutched to her chest. 'Joe,

stop sneaking up like that! You frightened the life
out of me!'

He chuckled and walked into the baby's bedroom,
joining her beside the changing mat, where MJ was lying
staring up at them with huge brown eyes. 'Is she giving
you a lecture, son?' he crooned, and picked the gurgling
baby up in his arms. MJ rewarded him by burping and
bringing up a dollop of curdled milk to decorate the
shoulder of his suit jacket.

'Thanks, mate,' Joe said mildly. 'Think that'll smell
better, do you?'

MJ bubbled and grinned happily.

'No social conscience. I blame the mother.' He handed
the baby back to her and blotted his jacket with a tissue.
'All set?'

She nodded, trying to ignore the butterflies that were
attacking her stomach.

'Got the milk?'

She nodded again. She had hired an electric breast-
pump to express her own milk for MJ to be given during
the day, and would go down to the nursery during her
lunch break to feed him as well. If she was really lucky
he wouldn't need her at other times. If.

She didn't really feel she'd have a prayer of his being
that co-operative, and wondered how reasonable and
accommodating Joe would be if she was called out of
an emergency Caesarean section to breast-feed her baby!
Well, they'd find out soon enough, she had no doubt.

Joe loaded his car with all the paraphernalia that MJ
needed for a day out, then Thea checked her appearance
once more in the mirror, blew herself a kiss just for good
luck and went out to the car with the baby.

Joe was waiting. 'Are you OK?' he asked softly as they got into the car and set off.

She nodded. 'Fine.' She wasn't. She was far from fine. She was nervous, dreading doing something stupid in a new department and messing up her relationship with Joe. It was already strained to capacity, she felt. She was worried about MJ. She was worried about Joe's colleagues and how they would take to her, and how she would get on, and what new challenges would face her.

Strange. Before she'd had the year out she had been brimming with confidence. Each new ward had been seen as a challenge, each new discipline as a reward for progress. Now she felt overwhelmed, lacking in confidence, incompetent.

She had become just a mother—if such a fundamentally important thing could be 'just' anything. She didn't feel she was a doctor any more. She felt light years from clinic practice, and she was terrified.

They pulled up in the hospital car park and she drew a deep, steadying breath.

'You can do it, Tink.' His voice was firm and full of assurance, and although she didn't believe him she was grateful for his support.

She turned and smiled at him, and if it was a bit wobbly he was kind enough not to mention it. 'Yes,' she said, trying to inject a little firmness into her voice. 'Yes, I can do it.'

Joe helped her unload MJ and gear into the crèche, and then, dragging her away, he went with her up to the maternity unit.

Jenny was on duty and greeted her with a hug. 'Hi! It's great to see you—I'm so glad it's you and not some hyperactive nail-biting youth with halitosis!'

Thea laughed, as she was meant to, and Joe led her to his office, found her a coat that fitted and then, just as he was about to open the door, he pulled her into his arms and hugged her.

'You'll be fine, sweetheart,' he murmured. 'In ten minutes you'll feel as if you've been here for ever.'

He was right. By lunchtime she had been to Theatre with Joe for an emergency Caesarean, helped with a ventouse delivery using a flexible suction cup instead of forceps to enhance a tired woman's own expulsive efforts, watched Joe repair a perineal tear and clerked a new admission without doing anything wrong—she hoped.

It was simply a case of following the instructions, but obviously with experience there would be other questions to ask as well, follow-ons from some of the answers. That was just a question of time, though, and there was only one way to deal with that and that was to let it happen.

She went down to the crèche and fed MJ during her break, studying him minutely to see if there was anything wrong with him, and yet again she told Angela about his theft when only a day old. 'You will watch him like a hawk, won't you?' she asked anxiously.

Angela laughed. 'Security's very tight,' she repeated. 'All the children are electronically tagged when they come in and the bands are removed by a machine when they go out. They simply can't be stolen.'

Thea checked the bracelet on MJ's arm, and smiled weakly. 'I'm just neurotic.'

'No, you're a mother. Now go on and have something to eat before you go back.'

She should, she thought, but there wasn't really time. She'd see if she could buy a bar of chocolate off the newspaper stand in the entrance.

She would have been able to if she'd had any money on her, but then she realised that her bag was locked in Joe's desk and she was empty-handed. Oh, well, she'd survive. Perhaps she'd lose some of those extra pounds that had sneaked on since she'd had the baby.

She went back up to the ward and found that there had been two new admissions that needed clerking. One of them was in for an elective Caesarean section, the other was in labour. Thea went to her first, flicking through the notes quickly on her way in.

'Hi,' she said brightly as she went into the little single room where the woman was lying on the bed, still dressed.

She was fine-boned and dark-haired, her brown eyes wide and watchful in her delicate face. The man with her was standing staring out of the window, one arm braced against the frame, his shoulders rigid. He turned at her entrance and met her eyes, and she saw the worry etched in them.

She held out her hand to each of them in turn. 'I'm Thea Stow, Mr Armitage's SHO. I just want to ask a few questions and have a look at you, Mrs Jones. Would you like your husband to stay or go?'

'Stay,' they said in unison.

She smiled. 'OK.' She perched on the edge of the bed and rested her clipboard on her knee. 'We'll just go through this quickly so I can check the details, and then the midwife will come and have a look at you and assess your progress. I see this is your second baby—any problems with the first?'

The couple exchanged meaningful glances. 'Laura lost the baby some years ago, almost at term. It should be in the notes.'

His voice was a little hard, and Thea cursed herself for not having looked more thoroughly before she came in. 'I'm sorry,' she said quietly. 'I only glanced at the notes. I should have studied them more closely. Could you tell me what the problem was?'

'Placental insufficiency.'

'I worked too hard for too long,' the woman added, and Thea could tell from the sadness still in her voice that this was a wound that would never really heal. She opened the notes, flicking through them quickly.

'You've been scanned?' she confirmed.

'Yes—regularly.'

'Any problems with this pregnancy? Anything you're worried about?'

They shook their heads. 'She's been resting,' the man said.

'Going crazy.'

They exchanged loving looks, and Thea could tell he had been fondly over-protective and probably a touch smothering in his love. The woman didn't seem to mind, though, and the baby was still very active, as she could see from the shifting contours of Mrs Jones's abdomen, so clearly his caution had not been in vain.

She was just completing her check-list and was about to examine the woman when the door opened behind her and Joe came in.

'Gavin—Laura. I've just heard you're here. How's it going?'

Thea looked at him in surprise. Did he greet all new arrivals so familiarly?

Gavin smiled, the tension in his blue eyes dissolving a little, and Laura's face relaxed.

'Hello, Joe,' Gavin said warmly. 'Everything's OK— a little on the drag, but not much. Your SHO was just clerking Laura.'

Joe shot her a glance and grinned encouragingly. 'Managing OK?'

'Sort of,' she said with a shrug. Her blunder over the stillborn baby was huge in her mind, and she wanted to apologise again, but she couldn't.

Joe sent her to clerk the other admission, and then found her just as she'd finished. She seized the opportunity to tell him about her *faux pas*.

'I feel so dreadful,' she told him. 'I should have checked the notes much more thoroughly.'

'Yes, you should have done, but you didn't, and there's no real harm done. I don't imagine your innocent blunder could make a great deal of difference to Laura's suffering. I should forget it and move on, but learn from it.'

'I will,' Thea said fervently.

'Anyway,' Joe continued, 'I should have warned you—everybody here knows about it. Gavin's a surgical registrar, Laura's a staff nurse, or she was until she became pregnant. Gavin insisted she gave up work the second they found out because of what happened last time. She was working right up to thirty-seven weeks when she had the baby, but it was already dead. The placenta was in appalling condition. Gavin was determined it wouldn't happen again this time.'

'I hope everything goes well.'

'We'll make sure it does,' Joe said, and his voice was full of quiet conviction. Thea didn't doubt for a moment that he would move heaven and earth to make sure it did.

Laura's labour progressed slowly. By the time the end of the day came, she was still in the very early stages. In view of her history, though, and to soothe her anxiety, she was to stay in hospital and be connected to a foetal monitor while she was resting, but since it was non-essential she could have it disconnected to use the bathroom or walk around.

Gavin stayed with her, and nothing could persuade him to leave.

'She might need me,' he said simply, and so he remained by her side, reading to her and telling her funny stories and sometimes just holding her hand while she slept.

Joe told the ward to contact him if there was any change or if they were concerned about anything, then he went with Thea down to the crèche and they collected Michael and all his paraphernalia.

He was hungry but quite safe, and they strapped him into his carry-cot in the car and drove home to the sound of his indignant cries.

'You feed him, I'll unload the car,' Joe told her, and she took the yelling infant into the kitchen, pulled up her soft knit shirt and unfastened her bra, then with the baby happily suckling she filled the kettle with one hand and plugged it in, then emptied the teapot, found some tea-bags and put milk into two mugs.

As she was pouring the tea Joe came into the kitchen, glanced at her and then the tea and said calmly, 'I hope that's cow's milk in the tea.'

She chuckled and threw a piece of stale toast at him. 'I wouldn't give you my milk anyway,' she said pertly. 'Much too good for the likes of you.'

His smile was a little off-centre. 'Probably curdle in the tea.'

'Actually it doesn't. I remember doing neonatal paediatrics—we ran out of milk on the ward one night and there was some leftover breast milk in the fridge. The staff nurse put it in our tea and didn't tell us till afterwards. It tasted fine.'

Joe glanced down at her breast, almost concealed by the hem of the shirt and the baby's mouth and hand, and turned away sharply. Heat streaked the back of his neck with dull red, and Thea could have kicked herself for embarrassing him yet again. Why did she always seem to feed the baby so publicly? Every time she did Joe seemed awkward about it.

Of course he was too kind and polite to tell her to go upstairs and do it out of his way. Hell, she must be wreaking havoc in his life.

'Think I'll take him upstairs and change him and give him a bath,' she said now, suddenly desperate to get out of Joe's way. 'Supper's in the fridge. I did it yesterday. It just needs to go into a hot oven for twenty minutes or so.'

And she fled, tea in hand, the baby still feeding peacefully while his mother vowed never to feed him out of her room again.

She bathed and changed him, then slipped him into his cot and watched as his little eyelids drooped shut and he went out like a light. After the quiet house the nursery was probably rather noisy, and no doubt he had had less sleep than he was used to.

Thea had a quick shower, pulled on some baggy cotton trousers and a sloppy sweatshirt and went back downstairs. As she entered the kitchen Joe slid a glass of wine towards her along the worktop.

'Here,' he said. 'Celebrate the end of your first day back in the fold.'

'Oh, thanks.' It was white, cold and refreshing, and it slipped down like silk. 'Gorgeous. Just what I needed—how did you know?'

He laughed. 'Mind-reader. And I fancied one too.' He raised his glass to her silently, winked and took a cooling sip. 'Mmm. Hits the spot. So, Dr Stow, how was your day?'

'OK apart from my howler.'

Joe shook his head. 'No howler. They're both in the profession; they know how it is.'

'And how is it?' Thea asked. 'Doctors too busy to check notes? That's how mistakes get made, Joe. It could have been much worse. What if she had been unconscious and a diabetic?'

'But she wasn't, and if she had been you would have searched the notes for a clue. Look, Thea, I admire your concern for perfection but I think you're getting worried about nothing. If you're still concerned, talk to Gavin tomorrow and apologise to him again.'

She swirled her wine. 'Do you think I should?'

'No. I think you did the right thing when you apologised at the time. Just make sure it doesn't happen again.'

'It won't.'

'Fine.'

And that was it, end of subject. They ate supper, a casserole with a layer of thinly sliced potatoes on top scattered with grated cheese, followed by fresh fruit, and Thea was more than ready for it. By the time they had finished clearing away in the kitchen she was also ready for bed. It had been a difficult day, and she was out of the routine.

'I think I'll go up,' she told him.

He nodded. 'OK. I'll be in the study if you want me.'

If she wanted him? Oh, yes, she wanted him. She wanted nothing more than to put her head against his chest and feel those strong arms around her, and lift her head for his kiss. She let her eyes linger for a fraction of a second on his firm, beautifully sculpted lips, and allowed herself the luxury of wondering how they would feel against hers.

Then with a muttered remark about a bath she turned on her heel and ran up the stairs to her room, shutting the door and leaning back against it. This was going to be harder than ever if her imagination was going to gang up on her too. It was bad enough enduring the things he did, without fantasising about the things she wanted him to do! If she started down that road again she'd go stark, staring crazy in no time flat.

She'd always idolised him. Then, as she'd grown older and he'd matured, he had become her secret fantasy whenever she'd allowed herself to think about it. Now, though, she was a widow with a tiny baby, sharing Joe's house. It was hardly an appropriate time to come on to him!

And it wouldn't make any difference anyway because,

for all he liked the baby, her presence in his house was clearly making him uncomfortable.

Three months, she told herself. Just three months, then she could go and leave him in peace, and lick her wounds elsewhere.

The thought was staggeringly painful. . .

There was no call in the night about Laura Jones. When Thea woke in the morning she made some tea and took a cup in to Joe and asked him, but he said there was no change. He'd rung at one on his way to bed and again in the night at about five, but she was fine, the baby was doing OK and there was very slow but steady progress.

'We might have to hurry her up,' he said, struggling into a sitting position and taking the tea from Thea.

Her eyes widened slightly and she headed for the door. 'I have to see to Michael—sorry to desert you,' she said with only a element of truth. Damn the man and his body! It wasn't fair that he should be so well made, and he shouldn't sleep in the buff like that!

She showered quickly and came out to hear the phone ringing. Joe's shower was running, so she answered the phone and then tapped on his door. 'Hospital—about Laura,' she told him.

He yanked open the bathroom door and took the phone from her, and once again she was face to face with his body, clad only in a hastily wrapped towel. His hair was wet, rivers streaming down his chest and over the firm washboard of his abdomen to be absorbed by the soft fabric of the towel. She wanted to take the towel and blot him dry, inch by glorious inch—

'Fine, thanks,' he said and cut off the connection, then handed Thea the phone.

'Laura's making progress. Nothing dramatic, but I don't want to hang about. Do you mind if we leave a bit early? We can have breakfast at the hospital once we've checked her, but this is one delivery I don't intend to miss.'

'Sure—fine,' she muttered, and, gathering her scattered wits, she ran back to her room, flung on her own clothes and dealt with the baby in double-quick time.

She was ready almost as soon as Joe, and he left her unloading the baby's things and taking them to the crèche while he went straight up to the ward to check on things.

By the time she arrived Laura had been moved to the delivery room, and she discovered that Joe had requested her presence.

She pulled on her coat, washed her hands and went into the room where Laura and Gavin were. It was the 'technical' delivery room, the one where problems usually ended up, and for a moment Thea thought things must have gone wrong.

Gavin, tired but still cheerful, smiled at her.

'Morning,' she said, returning his smile, and moved to Joe's side.

'I gather you wanted me in here?' she said softly.

'Mmm. I thought it would be nice for you to see a normal delivery. If you aren't careful you end up like the cavalry, and some obstetricians never get to see a normal birth. If you're going into general practice you need to know what's normal to start with.'

'Doesn't Laura mind?' she murmured.

'No. She's too busy watching the baby monitor.'

Thea's eyes flicked to it. 'But it looks OK, doesn't it? No problems?'

'None at all, but it's rather like you and MJ and security—she just wants to be sure.'

Thea could understand that absolutely. 'What do you want me to do?' she asked.

'Nothing. Just be here, help if you're asked to and call me if you panic. I'll be in my office—I've got some paperwork to do. Oh, and shout just before the end—I'd like to see this baby born.'

Bev Linari, the midwife, laughed at his words. 'Go on, Joe, out. We don't need you.'

He went, reluctantly, and Thea turned to Laura. 'Hi. How is it?'

The woman smiled wanly. 'OK, I suppose. It's been a long, quiet night. I woke up at six with something that could have been a contraction, but nothing much happened till I went to the loo. I think it must have been walking round that did it.'

'I wanted to walk round but I couldn't,' Thea told her. 'I was on my own with Joe the night of the storm, back in February. We had to cope on our own, and he couldn't support me and catch the baby all at the same time. I felt cheated, in a way.'

Laura looked at the monitor and sighed. 'I want to walk round, but I feel I should be here connected to this thing. There's a portable one but it's unreliable apparently.' She chewed her lip, and Thea exchanged a meaningful look with Bev.

'You don't need it, my love,' Bev told her softly. 'You could manage quite well without it. Your baby's fine. It's shown no sign of distress so far, you're progressing quite well and I can check the heartbeat every time you have a contraction. If you feel insecure and want to have the monitor back on, you can, at any time. Just try without.'

Laura turned to her husband. 'Gavin?' she whispered.

'Do whatever you like. I think Bev's right, sweetheart. I'm sure the baby's fine, but if it worries you too much, stay where you are.'

'But I want to walk round!' Laura said, clearly distressed by her dilemma.

'Then walk round, and Bev will check regularly, and we'll all be here, and if anything starts to look iffy you'll be sorted out in a flash.' He gave her a gentle hug. 'You'll be fine, darling. Really.'

She was. Summoning the courage to allow Bev to disconnect the machine, she slid her feet to the floor and walked round, supported by Gavin on one side and Bev on the other. Every time she had a contraction Bev checked the baby's heartbeat while Thea held Laura up, and after a few normal contractions with no reported problems she told Bev she had the urge to push.

'Do you want to lie down, or keep walking?' Bev asked her.

She hesitated, and Thea recognised the enormity of her trust in Bev when she said she'd keep walking.

'Could you get Joe, Thea?' Bev asked her, and she popped her head round the door and hailed Jenny who was at the nurses' station.

She promised to phone Joe in his office, and Thea went back to her task of helping to support Laura while Bev checked the baby's progress.

'Lovely, steady descent,' she reported. 'Still happy walking round?'

'I want to squat, I think,' Laura said, panting a little. 'Oh, hell, I really have to push.'

She began to crouch, and Gavin got behind her, his arms under her armpits, letting her hang on him so she could concentrate on what was happening rather than trying to balance.

'It's coming,' Bev warned. 'Just pant, my love—that's it, nice and steady. Don't push. The head's nearly out—gosh, what a lot of hair. Oh, yes, baby, hello!'

The head was delivered, and Thea watched, fascinated, as it turned in Bev's hands and the shoulders slipped out, one after the other, followed by the rest of the baby. As the cool air met its skin, the little arms and legs drew up in horror and the baby let out a blood-curdling scream of rage.

Bev lifted the baby, Gavin lowered Laura to a hastily positioned mat on the floor and then, as Thea watched, Bev placed the baby in her mother's waiting arms.

'You've got a little girl,' she told them, and Thea saw Laura's eyes close in a mixture of grief and joy. Gavin gathered his wife and child tenderly into his arms, and Thea saw the trail of tears on his cheek as he turned his head. What a bitter-sweet moment, she thought, and swallowed a huge lump in her throat.

She looked away to give Laura and Gavin some privacy, and saw Joe standing there watching them, his eyes bright.

Him too? She moved to his side. 'Everything was fine,' she told him, and then huge tears sploshed over and landed on her coat.

Joe's thumbs came up and smudged them away. 'Softy,' he said gruffly.

'You can talk.'

He grinned, a little off-kilter. 'There's just something about childbirth that strips away pretence. It gets me every time. I'm glad it gets you too.'

Thea smiled weakly. 'It could be a real handicap. People will think I'm nuts.'

'Rubbish,' he chided. 'Look at Bev.'

She was bustling about, doing the things that needed doing, but as she turned towards them Thea could see the black spikes of her lashes clumped together.

'After all the babies she's seen delivered?'

'Even so. Come on, let's leave them in peace. We can come back in a little while.'

He led her out, took her to his office and gave her a cup of coffee. 'Right,' he said as she finished it. 'We're doing a clinic today. That means you go in front of me and do a preliminary check on all the mums, then I follow and see those that need my personal attention.'

'Who decides?' she asked.

'I do. Everyone gets a quick chat, those with history get more close attention. Anything you turn up that seems unusual you bring to my attention, even if it's just a hunch—and Thea?'

She looked at him and saw the teasing glint in his eyes.

'Read the notes?' she suggested.

He grinned.

CHAPTER SIX

IN THE end Joe took Thea under his wing for the majority of that first clinic, once he was happy that Laura Jones was OK and didn't need his attention. Having been a patient herself recently, Thea was used to the routine, but even so she was glad of his presence and watched carefully to see what he did and how he did it.

The first thing he always did was shake the patient by the hand, a practice which Thea found had been lacking in her personal obstetric experience, and which she was sure helped to put the women at their ease. That was something he seemed very good at, she noticed, and it was astonishing at times how much the patients would relax and begin to laugh and really communicate with him. He would refer to the notes from time to time, but he clearly knew the contents pretty thoroughly, and her own lapse seemed even more enormous in the light of his clinical practice.

The examinations were always last, after he had chatted and observed and checked the recent history and any results of tests which might have been done—scans, bloods and so forth. His examination was gentle and thorough, and he often included Thea.

'Feel this—what a lovely presentation,' or, 'The baby's lying with its feet out—is that so it can kick your husband better? Feel this, Dr Stow. A footballer in the making!'

After that one, he explained to her that unless the baby turned round the mother would have more difficulty with her labour as the face would be to the front—face to pubes, or occipito-posterior, as it was also called.

'Will she need a forceps delivery?' Thea asked.

He shrugged. 'Maybe. Careful, scrupulous management and continuous reassessment, certainly, and if she gets into difficulties then she may need help, but I'd go for the ventouse with a soft silicone rubber cup as the instrument of choice for causing the least damage. Depends on the presentation of the face and the mother's condition. I'd keep her up and going as long as possible—all the way through if I could.'

'Even with the ventouse?'

'Certainly.' Joe grinned. 'It's a technique I learned from William Parry. He's known by the midwives as Dr Ventouse because of the skill with which he uses it. He's an excellent teacher too.'

They moved on to the next patient, and as Thea worked alongside him, gradually assuming more responsibility and performing more of the routine tasks, she wondered why she had felt so nervous yesterday morning.

As they left one patient on the way to another, Joe grinned at her. 'Getting quite the old hand, aren't you?'

She smiled back. 'I feel as if I've been here for ages.'

'Good. What did I tell you? And next week you can show me how good you are at needlework, if we get an obliging perineum or two. Three, preferably, so I can show you twice and then you can do your own.'

'Do the midwives do their own suturing?' she asked, to clear up a point that had puzzled her.

'Depends. If there's a doctor already involved, usually

not. It also depends on the midwife, the extent of the tear or cut and any reported problems from previous deliveries. Sometimes, if things have gone wrong before, following a tear I'll try and sort out the mess there and then, to make sure it doesn't happen again, but long complicated repairs without a general anaesthetic can be very uncomfortable and tiring for the woman.'

'So do you give a GA?'

'If I can't avoid it. I hesitate to give GAs without real need because of the increased risk to the patient, so it really is a case of taking each individual in turn and making a clinical decision on the findings. The midwife certainly wouldn't be expected to suture anything very complex or long-winded, and anyway they often don't have time if there's another delivery demanding their attention.'

She shot him a wry look. 'And you do?'

He laughed. 'Sometimes. Not often. Making time is the thing I do best.' He then proceeded to do exactly that, after she had had lunch and fed MJ, dragging Thea with him on an endless round of operations, check-ups and emergency deliveries.

By the end of the day she was even more impressed by his skill than she had been before. The awkward, diffident boy she had known as a child was a different person from the Joe she was now getting to know. The man he had become was decisive, thoughtful, reasonable, confident and highly skilled, someone in whom one could have the utmost faith, both personally and professionally.

She watched his technique with the ventouse, and saw him deliver a baby while the woman squatted, arms draped over the head of the bed, and her pelvic outlet increased some thirty per cent by the position. He had already attached the suction cup to the baby's head with the woman lying down, and even that had looked difficult enough to Thea.

However, the diameter of the pelvic outlet had obviously still been causing problems, and so he and the midwife had helped her up into her squatting position.

With a twist and a wriggle, he managed to coax the head down, and, working with her contractions, he and the midwife orchestrated a careful delivery that left the woman with nothing more than a minor perineal graze to show for the birth of her very healthy baby.

Thea was very impressed.

She was also shattered. It was the end of her second day, and the start of what would be a long weekend because of the May Day holiday on Monday. Another firm was on call, and she could go home and spend three glorious days with her feet up, resting and enjoying her baby before going back to work on Tuesday. She could hardly wait.

They picked MJ up from the crèche, and after piling all his stuff in the car they set off for home. On the way Thea considered what they might have for supper, and her heart sank at the thought of feeding and bathing MJ, cooking and clearing up, tackling the inevitable washing and generally tidying up before she could sit down. Joe, as usual, seemed to read her thoughts.

'Fancy a take-away?' he suggested.

She laughed. 'Will you stop second-guessing me?'

He grinned. 'Don't have to be much of a soothsayer to see you're shattered, Tink,' he told her fondly. 'I am too. Been one of those busy, busy days.'

It had—very busy. Thea reflected on all she had learned, and was amazed she had only been there two days. It seemed like far longer. They picked up a pizza smothered in stretchy cheese and masses of extra toppings, and didn't even bother to unload the car before taking it into the kitchen to eat it.

At least, that was the theory. Just as Thea sank her teeth into the first bite, MJ woke up and started yelling for his next feed.

'Keep mine hot; I'll quickly feed him,' she said, and, scooping him up, she headed for the stairs.

'Feed him here while you eat,' Joe called after her.

She turned, looking back at him, searching his face for any sign of awkwardness, but there was none.

'Are you sure?'

'Of course,' he mumbled round a mouthful. Strings of cheese dangled from his lips and he flicked his tongue out and retrieved them. A strange shiver went through Thea.

Almost reluctantly, she went back into the kitchen and sat down at the table, unfastened her bra and lifted her shirt just far enough to latch the baby on. There was instant, blissful silence, broken only by the steady sucking noise MJ made as he fed.

Joe watched her for a moment, then his eyes slid away and he cleared his throat, pushing the pizza box towards her. 'Come on, eat up.'

She took a slice and nibbled it, watching Joe from under her lashes. Was he embarrassed? No. Maybe. No—oh, hell, she didn't know and she didn't care. It was his fault she was in the kitchen; let him deal with his feelings. She took a bigger bite of the pizza and shut her eyes. Bliss.

*   *   *

Joe watched her eat, stunned by how much he cared for the woman and child that were sharing his life. She was exhausted, he could see that, the unaccustomed routine killing after such a long break.

She was shaping up, though. She had a lot to learn, obviously, but she wasn't afraid to admit her mistakes. That was Thea, though. She'd always been like that.

He stole another glance at the baby, whose small fist clutched a handful of Thea's shirt, his face turned into his mother's breast. All Joe could see was the little jaw working busily as he suckled, and he turned away again, taking another slice of pizza and swivelling round to put his feet up on another chair, so the scene wasn't directly in front of him.

He found the cosy little scene a bit much to cope with. It made him feel awkward and unnecessary and excluded, and he was desperately conscious that this was an area of MJ's care that he was unable to help with.

'Uncle Joe?'

Perhaps not entirely. With a slow smile he reached out and took the baby from her, propped him up against his shoulder and waited for the burp. He wasn't disappointed. Seconds later the baby was rooting for the next half, his little mouth pecking softly at Joe's neck and demolishing his poise.

'Here,' he said gruffly, handing the baby back to his mother, and without a word he walked out of the room, ran upstairs and stripped off his clothes before walking into the shower.

They were going to leave him. He knew it would happen, and getting her the job had simply trapped her with him for another three months, but when the months were up, what would he do then? How would he entice her to stay longer?

He thought of the house before they had come, and realised that it wouldn't feel like that again. It would be empty as it had never been empty before.

How the hell would he cope with that? God only knows.

He turned off the shower, snagged a towel from the rail and walked out into his bedroom, blotting his arms and chest absently. Then he looked up to see Thea on the landing, MJ in her arms, transfixed.

Her eyes flicked up to his, she blushed furiously and with a muttered apology she almost ran into MJ's room. Joe sighed, shut the door and sat on the bed. Damn. The last thing he needed to do was drive her out. In future he'd be more careful to shut the door...

Thea had a wonderful lie-in on Saturday morning. She woke early to feed MJ, but, bless his heart, he went straight back to sleep, and she did too. Joe went out at some point, and she woke up long enough to register the sound of his car leaving the drive. Nothing else penetrated until MJ cried again at nearly eleven, so she fed him again, bathed him and put him in his bouncy cradle to watch her while she bathed.

She dressed in comfy, casual clothes, then went down to have a poke about in the freezer. She was just assembling the ingredients for their evening meal when Joe wandered through the back door.

'Oh!' she exclaimed. 'I thought you were out.'

'Planning a secret feast?' he asked with a grin,

studying the piles of food on the worktop.

'Supper,' she told him. 'And don't be rude or you won't get any.'

He delved his hand into his pocket and pulled out an envelope. 'Will it keep? Gavin gave me tickets for tonight's May Ball at the town hall—it's a dinner dance. I thought we could go, if you don't mind leaving MJ with Gavin.'

'Gavin?' she said, her eyes widening.

'He offered. He knows we can't go out without a babysitter, so he volunteered.'

She blinked, still trying to adjust to the idea of a ball. 'I haven't got anything to wear—'

'So go and get something.'

She blinked again and shook her head to clear it. 'Why did he give you the tickets?'

'Because Laura's not going to be in a position to attend.'

She rolled her eyes at him. 'I know that. I just wondered why they bought the tickets in the first place.'

'They didn't—they won a raffle prize.'

She chewed her lip. She'd love to go. She hadn't been out since—oh, since Mike. More than a year. Almost eighteen months. It seemed like for ever, and suddenly she really badly wanted to go out.

'I wonder if I've got anything to wear?' she murmured.

'Buy something.'

'I can't afford to, Joe.'

'But I can.'

She shook her head. 'No. I feel enough of a kept woman as it is.'

He tried another tack. 'Let me give you the money I

would have had to spend on the tickets to put towards a dress.'

She hesitated, and he clucked and told her to get the baby ready.

'What for?'

'We're going to town to find you some glad rags— come on.'

She tried to resist, but not very hard, and not for long. The lure was too great, the temptation to dress up and look beautiful again too much after such a long time. She was beginning to feel so dowdy—oh, why not? It was only money. . .

She found a dress in the third shop Joe took her to. A lovely subdued kingfisher-blue, the dress was made of a silk mixture and draped like a dream. It felt wonderful, so soft, and the cowl neck scooped discreetly over her now more generous bust.

Conscious of MJ starting up a demanding yodel, she glanced quickly in the mirror, happy that the fabric didn't do anything too terrible to her bottom or tummy, and satisfied that the folds of the cowl neck could be arranged to draw attention away from the devastation pregnancy had wrought on her body. MJ's screaming made up her mind. It was this one or nothing.

She bought it, accepting Joe's contribution towards the cost without another murmur. She would simply add it to the ever mounting debt. Hastening back to the car, conscious of the seeping dampness in her bra caused by her natural maternal reaction to her baby's hunger, she surreptitiously pressed the heel of her hand against first one nipple, then the other, to try and stop the reflex.

Joe, ever perceptive, noticed immediately. 'You can feed him in the car,' he murmured. 'Only another minute or two. Is it very uncomfortable?'

She laughed awkwardly. 'No—just a nuisance. I only have to think about feeding him and my let-down reflex works, like a well-trained dairy cow.'

He chuckled. 'I'll have to start calling you Daisy.'

'That's the breast-pump. I took the portable one back—they've got one in the crèche I can use.'

He opened the car door for her, passed her the baby when she was in and then busied himself collapsing the buggy and putting the shopping in the boot while she fed MJ. The front of the car was facing the car-park wall, and it was quite discreet. No one could see her except Joe.

'Well, if he gets embarrassed he'll just have to deal with it,' she muttered as he got in the car.

'Problems?'

'No. Just chuntering. Ignore me.'

He sat back, arms folded over his broad chest, staring out of the windscreen.

'So,' he said finally, 'how do you think your job's going to work out? Will you manage to juggle MJ and the hours all right?'

She shot him a quick glance. Was she supposed to say yes, or no? Whichever was the truth, she decided immediately. This was Joe, not some mindless bureaucrat who needed his ego pandering to.

'Yes, I think I'll manage, but feeding him could become a problem.'

'No. You keep struggling, and I'll cover you if you have to go and feed him.'

'And if there's a time when I can't struggle?'

'Then I'll make another arrangement. So long as there's a genuine need I don't see why we can't be flexible.'

'And what about when you feel I should have more responsibility and you want me to cover the nights?'

He gave her a strange look. 'Let's worry about that if and when we get to it.'

'Well, of course we'll get to it!' she exclaimed. 'I can leave milk at home, but I can hardly expect you to get up and feed him, then bring him into the hospital!'

'Don't worry,' he soothed again. 'By the time you're working nights he'll be older, going through the night and much easier to deal with.'

'And if he's not?'

'Then I'll do your nights.'

Thea opened her mouth to argue, then shut it again. One thing she had learned about Joe in the past three months was that when he used that tone of voice, you might as well bash your head against a brick wall. He redefined the word 'stubborn' with a vengeance.

'We'll see,' she muttered, determined not to give in.

'Yes, we will,' he said easily, and reached across to take MJ away from her ineffectual patting. He sat him on the steering wheel, looked him in the eye and said, 'Burp, please,' then smiled in satisfaction. 'Right on cue—good lad. What a lovely little lager lout you're going to be.'

Thea rearranged her clothes hastily, opened her door and took the baby from him, tucking Michael securely into his carry-cot with the straps on.

'Right, home,' she said firmly. 'If I have to go out tonight looking like anything at all, I need to put in some serious time in front of the mirror.'

Joe's snort could have meant anything.

The town hall was floodlit, and as Thea and Joe
approached it on foot they could see the other party-goers
arriving in their finery.

Thea was suddenly, desperately glad she had given in
and bought a new dress. Not that she'd had a proper look
at it yet, of course, because just as she had been putting
it on MJ had started to scream with colic and she had
had to try and soothe him before Gavin arrived to babysit.

The wrap she had flung round her shoulders was
cream, a lovely contrast to the dress, and a perfect colour
for another of MJ's burpy little offerings as they'd left
the house. She had blotted it dry, terribly glad it hadn't
been Joe's dinner suit, and rushed out to the car after
him, hardly sparing him a glance.

Now, as they entered the foyer and she surrendered
her wrap to the cloakroom attendant, she turned and
looked at Joe properly for the first time, and her heart
jammed in her throat.

It seemed that the man who could look good in a towel
and a few drops of water could look mind-bendingly
devastating in a formal dinner suit. The cut was superb,
and she was immediately overwhelmingly conscious of
him. Dear God, would she be able to hide her feelings
during this long evening together? It was the first time
they had done anything that might move their relationship
out of the brother/sister slot it had occupied for the past
twenty years, and Thea felt suddenly terribly vulnerable.

She looked up and met his eyes, and was startled to
see him staring at her as if transfixed. 'What's wrong?'

she whispered. 'Have I spilt something down my front?'

He gave a strangled laugh. 'No, but you might as well have done, the looks you'll attract.'

She looked down, horrified. 'What's wrong? Does it look awful? I knew I didn't have the figure for it—'

'Thea, if it looked any better on you you simply wouldn't be safe.' His voice softened. 'You look stunning, Tink. Beautiful. I was just admiring you.'

She looked up, surprised by the husky tone of his voice, and saw a territorial pride in his eyes. She smiled, a woman's smile, and laid her hand against his chest. 'You're no slouch yourself,' she told him. 'Come on, Armitage. Show me a good time. I haven't had fun in ages, and I don't think you have either. Let's party.'

They did, dancing and eating and laughing and having fun, and as the emcee announced the last waltz Joe drew Thea into his arms for the slow number.

Her head found a natural spot on his shoulder, his hand warm against the small of her back, holding her against his chest. Their legs meshed, moving in perfect time, and beneath her ear Thea could hear the steady, even rhythm of his heart.

She turned her head so that her face was close to his neck, the slight stubble of his jaw rough against her forehead. He had splashed on aftershave, something citrusy and clean, and under it she could just detect the faint scent of his skin, masculine but indefinable. If she could bottle that, she thought wildly, she could make millions.

Someone collided with her and she stumbled against him, and instantly his hand on her back tightened, holding her more firmly against him.

'OK?' he murmured.

She wasn't. Far from it. She could feel every inch of his body against hers, hot and hard and infinitely desirable. Her heart pounding, her breath jamming in her throat, she eased away a little.

'Fine,' she whispered shakily. 'I'm fine.'

She took a steadying breath, but it carried with it his own personal fragrance and her legs felt like jelly. She hadn't known she could feel like this—hadn't realised it was possible to want like this, to tremble and ache and yearn for someone to the exclusion of all common sense.

She wanted to drag him away from the seething crowd to a place where they could be alone, and there make love to him until they both wept for mercy. Instead she dropped her arms and stepped back.

'Perhaps we should go now before the crush starts,' she suggested, and he jumped at it.

Lord, she thought, either it's got to him too, or he's finding a slow dance with me too tedious for words.

His face gave nothing away, of course, and when she retrieved her wrap and they made their way out into the chilly evening he hurried her to the car to get her out of the freshening wind. They drove home in silence, and when they entered the hall they could hear MJ grizzling in the kitchen with Gavin rocking him helplessly.

'Oh, no!' Thea cried, rushing in. 'Gavin, I'm sorry— has he been awful?'

Gavin grinned. 'Just for the last half hour. I knew you wouldn't be long, though. I fed him again at ten, but I think he wants rather more.'

'Oh, sweetheart!' She took the baby from Gavin, hitched up her skirt and ran upstairs to her bedroom.

Laying him on the bed, she threw off her wrap and turned towards the wardrobe to hang up her dress, and as she did so she saw herself face on in the dress for the first time.

Her jaw dropped, and she laid a hand across her cleavage. Dear God! No wonder Joe had boggled and half the men in the room had spent the evening staring at her! And she'd assumed she'd looked good, instead of which she looked—well. . .

Good. She did look good. She looked beautiful, but sensual too, a woman in every sense of the word. She looked again at her cleavage, and moaned softly. Never, in all her life, had she owned something as revealing and outrageous as this.

MJ screamed again, and, forgetting the dress, she shucked it off, pulled on her dressing gown and perched at the top of the bed to feed him. A few moments later there was a tap on the door and Joe put his head round.

'I've brought you a cup of tea.'

'Bless you. Come on in.'

He had shed his jacket and the bow-tie dangled from the open collar of his dress shirt. He looked rumpled and sexy and good enough to eat, and Thea dragged her eyes away and looked down at the baby.

'He's ravenous. I didn't manage to express very much before we had to go out.'

Joe was silent, and after a moment she looked up to see him staring down at her and the baby. 'He's grown,' Joe said gruffly.

'He's nearly three months old. I can't believe I've been here that long, and yet it seems like for ever. I can hardly remember anything of the time after Mike died before I came to you. There's just a black fog.'

Joe sat on the end of the bed and looked back at her, a strange expression on his face. 'It's nearly a year now, isn't it?'

She nodded. 'On the second of June. It seems much longer.'

'You must miss him.'

She thought of the evening she had just spent with Joe, only eleven months after her husband had died; they had laughed and danced and she had wanted Joe so badly that she'd thought she would die. Miss Mike? She hadn't given him a single thought, and now it seemed indecent, disloyal, a terrible betrayal. She should be grieving still, focusing on his son, not dancing the night away in the arms of another man.

She lifted a shoulder in a helpless little shrug. 'It just seems so long ago. I can hardly even remember his voice. But it seems terribly, dreadfully wrong that Michael will never know his own father.'

Her voice cracked, staring down at her son, and she shut her eyes and shook her head in denial. Joe's hands were there then, easing her up against his shoulder, and for the first time she let herself cry for her son and the father he would never know.

Joe held her through the healing tears, and when she hiccuped to a halt he handed her a tissue, took the sleepy baby and winded him, then changed his nappy and settled him in his cot.

'Go to bed, Tink,' he said gently to her. 'It'll seem better in the morning.'

She smiled unsteadily. 'Maybe. Joe?'

He looked back. 'Yes, sweetheart?'

'Thanks for tonight.'

His mouth tightened a fraction, then he smiled. 'My pleasure, Tink. Thank *you*.' And with a little bow of his head and a comforting wink he left her alone with her guilt.

CHAPTER SEVEN

THE following morning Joe let Thea lie in. She fed MJ, of course, but both of them went back to sleep and it was only when the baby woke again at ten-thirty that Joe came in with a cup of tea and set it down beside her.

She was propped up against her pillows, the baby lying in the crook of her arm feeding happily. Joe hesitated a moment, then reached out and brushed his fingertips over the baby's head.

'His hair's growing—it's got a touch of red in it, like yours.' He drew his hand away, and Thea saw it tremble slightly before he pulled it back and went over to the window. He opened the curtains a little. 'It's a beautiful day,' he told her, his back still to her. 'Do you fancy a picnic?'

Fun in the sun? she thought. Another photo-opportunity for her guilty conscience? What a fine time to pick to start to feel bad about Mike's death. Then she thought of MJ and how it would be good for him to have some fresh air after being inside at the crèche for two days, and she weakened.

'That would be lovely. Do you want me to make some sandwiches?'

'We'll buy some on the way. Drink your tea and finish feeding MJ, and then I'll get him ready while you sort yourself out.'

It was wonderful having a built-in nanny, she thought.

Rather like a father for the baby. She handed MJ over, and as she saw Joe's face soften as he smiled down at her son her conscience pricked her yet again. Was it fair to him—to both of them—to allow them to get so attached to each other?

Joe's lonely, she told herself, and then wondered how much more lonely he would be when they left. It would be peaceful, yes, but how much peace could a person stand? Anyway, it was months hence. She'd have to wean them off each other.

She showered quickly, threw on light cotton trousers and a polo shirt with a cotton sweater in case it became chilly, and ran downstairs. Joe was in the kitchen, with MJ in his bouncy chair gurgling happily to himself and banging a rattle against the bar. As she went in Joe quirked a brow at her. 'All set?'

'I need a bag for MJ—'

'It's here.'

'Oh. Right, then, I'm ready—except for breakfast.'

He chucked her an apple from the fruit bowl. 'Here—munch this. We'll pick up sandwiches on the way and have lunch early.'

By the time they'd pulled up in a wooded area at the edge of an open heath and parked the car, Thea was starving.

'Let's walk over there a bit and put a rug down under that tree,' Joe suggested.

'Only if we can do it quickly before I fade away.'

Joe laughed. 'You won't fade. You're made of sterner stuff than that.' He handed her the baby and the rug, gathered up all the picnic stuff, the bag of MJ's bits and pieces and locked the car, then headed off across the heather towards the tree he had pointed out.

Thea trailed after him, her stomach screaming its protest, and as she arrived at the tree Joe took the blanket, spread it out half in the shade and took the baby from her. 'Go on, get stuck in. I can see you're desperate.'

She laughed. 'It's feeding him—he's so greedy now. I think I might have to start introducing some solids at three months. I know you aren't supposed to, but I don't really want to give him cow's milk formula yet and I don't think I've got enough milk.'

Joe's eyes flicked to her breasts and away again. 'Are you drinking enough?' he asked, and his voice was a little rough.

He's embarrassed again, she thought. Why do I have to keep either breastfeeding in front of him or talking about it?

'I drink loads,' she assured him. 'Now, about this food.'

Joe sat down with his back to the tree, the baby in the shade beside him on his back playing with his rattle, still perfectly content. Thea passed Joe a sandwich, then picked her own up in two hands and sank her teeth into the middle of it with enthusiasm.

The mayonnaise squirted out and dolloped onto her front, taking a prawn with it. Before she could move, Joe's hand darted out and stole the prawn. 'Hey!' she laughed. 'That was mine!'

Joe's eyes twinkled. 'Not any more.'

She glanced down at her front. 'Look at this mess!' she wailed. 'If it isn't the baby being sick on me I've thrown food all over myself. I'm not fit to take anywhere any more!'

Joe chuckled, and reaching over, he blotted the front of her polo shirt with one of the baby's tissues. 'Mucky pup,' he said affectionately, and then, as if he suddenly realised what he was doing, his hand seemed to go into slow motion and freeze, and he pulled it away, heat scorching his cheeks. 'Sorry,' he muttered, and withdrew back to his tree, leaving her sitting on the other edge of the rug.

Even so she could still feel the touch of his hand against her breast, and the thoughts it provoked made her own cheeks burn. She turned back to her sandwich, finishing it with great care and far more attention than it actually merited.

They finished the food almost in silence, exchanging the odd word here and there but for the most part ignoring each other and trying to banish wayward thoughts. At least Thea was. She had no idea what Joe was thinking. Embarrassed again by her ever present breasts. Damn. She was going to start wearing a liberty bodice, one of those terrible cotton things stitched with lines of tape that her mother had had as a child, impossible to get on and off and hideously confining.

Perhaps then Joe's sensibilities wouldn't be offended on quite such a regular basis.

The thought was so ludicrous that she laughed softly, and Joe turned to her.

'What?'

'Nothing. Is there any more food?'

Joe peered in the bag. 'A piece of squashed fruit cake.'

She wrinkled her nose up. 'No. I'll pass.' She glanced at the baby, fast asleep between them, and then, shifting, she stretched out in the sun on her back and pushed her unruly curls out of the way.

'Mind you don't burn.'

'I don't.'

'Everyone does in the end.'

'Joe, stop fussing.'

He muttered an apology and stood up, gathering rubbish together and putting it into the bag, then carrying it to the car. He came back and stood looking down at her. 'Are you OK for a minute? I fancy stretching my legs.'

Getting away from me, more like, before I embarrass you any more, Thea thought. 'I'm fine,' she assured him. 'You go ahead.'

He went, and because his advice was sensible and she knew he was right she moved so that her face and arms were in the shade. Her body was still warmed by the glorious sunshine, and in a few minutes she was asleep.

She didn't hear Joe come back, but when she opened her eyes he was there, his back against the tree again, watching MJ with a strange expression on his face.

'Hi,' she said softly. 'Nice walk?'

His eyes flicked to hers. 'Not bad.' He looked back at MJ again. 'Thea, can I ask you something personal?'

She struggled into a sitting position. Lying flat on her back like that, she felt too vulnerable somehow. She shoved her hair back and turned to face him. 'Sure—fire away.'

'What provision have you made for Michael in the event of your death?'

She blinked. Whatever she had expected, it hadn't been that. She gathered her scattered wits. 'Um—nothing. I hadn't thought about it.'

Joe looked awkward. 'I wondered—perhaps—would you consider making me his legal guardian in the event of anything happening to you? It's just—well, your parents are both gone now, you're an only child—there isn't really anyone else close to you, certainly no one else who knows him. And I know it isn't something you want to have to think about, but the unthinkable does happen and I couldn't bear him to end up with someone who didn't love him or didn't want him.'

'Like you did?' she said quietly.

He met her eyes then and the bleakness in his made her want to weep for him. 'Yes. Like I did.'

'Tell me about your uncle, Joe.'

He looked away again, pulling up a blade of grass and shredding it. His hands shook slightly. 'I was in the way. My parents had left some money to be used on my education and upbringing, but my uncle's children weren't in private schools and because I was they hated me. I interfered with the even tenor of their family life, I was difficult and awkward and unhappy, and they didn't know how to deal with me, so they didn't bother.

'They sent me to school, they fed me, and beyond that they ignored me. If I needed help with homework I was told that my flashy expensive school couldn't be much cop if they didn't teach me how to do things. Half the trouble was that I couldn't concentrate at school because I was so unhappy. After a while, though, it became the only place where I could be myself.'

'And my father was your housemaster.'

'Yes. If it hadn't been for John Reynolds I wouldn't be here now. I started talking to him, pouring out my heart, and he just listened and seemed to understand.

Then I got into the county cricket squad and my cousin didn't, and he and some of his friends took me on one side and beat me up. I got away and made my way to the school, and sheltered there overnight outside the labs where your father taught. He found me in the morning, half-frozen, battered and bruised, and he went to the police. I haven't seen any of them since.'

'That's when you came to us.'

He shook his head. 'No. I went to a foster family straight away, but they were very different. Kind, but light years away from what I was used to. I was safe but miserable, and your father went to social services and asked if I could live with him. They said yes.'

'And you had to put up with me trailing you and hero-worshipping and being a pain, and here I am still driving you mad.'

He laughed, breaking the tension, and tugged her hair gently. 'Here you are still, and I'm very glad to have you, Tink. Anyway, enough about me. Answer the question—or do you want to think about it?'

She shook her head. 'There's nothing to think about, Joe. I hope it isn't necessary, for obvious reasons, but I can't think of a single person I would rather have look after him. I know he'd be safe and happy with you. I know I can trust you.'

Their eyes locked for a moment, then she was in his arms, hugged hard against his broad, firm chest. 'Thanks for the vote of confidence, Tink.'

She squeezed him hard. 'Any time.' She couldn't say any more. Apart from the fact that he was crushing all the air out of her lungs, there was a lump in her throat the size of a house and words seemed to get stuck behind it.

He patted her awkwardly, then released her, ruffling her hair as if she were ten again. 'That's my girl,' he said gruffly. 'Hell, all this soul-baring and emotion! It's woken MJ.'

She eased away, blinking back the tears that blurred her eyes, and reached for the gurgling baby. 'Hello, darling,' she said gently. 'Had a lovely nap?' He snuggled into her side, instantly happy, and watched her with big brown eyes as she struggled for her composure.

She was unbearably touched by Joe's story, and by the fact that he wanted to be guardian to her beloved son. Blinking away tears, she waved the rattle for MJ and watched him reach for it, and thought how lucky she had been to be loved and wanted as a child—just as her own baby was loved and wanted.

And, thanks to Joe, always would be.

As her experience at work grew, so did Thea's responsibility. She was involved more and more with decision-making about difficult deliveries and whether or not to intervene, and on one occasion felt confident enough to go head to head with Joe.

The patient was in her early thirties, a fit and active woman with two previous pregnancies behind her. The first delivery had been normal and uneventful, if slow, the second had been a Caesarean for lack of progress— perhaps an extension of her slow but uneventful first delivery? Thea thought so, and felt she should have another chance.

'I think she should have a trial of labour,' she told Joe, after seeing her in the clinic when she was almost at term.

'On what grounds?'

'On the grounds that her second labour may have been misunderstood. Perhaps it was just very slow. If the baby was all right, she probably didn't need surgical intervention.'

He looked at her calmly. 'Have you checked the notes?'

She flushed. 'Of course.'

'And?'

'The decision to operate was made by Derek Blythe.'

Joe arched a brow. 'Really? I hadn't realised. She's always been a patient of this firm, though—she was under my predecessor.'

'She was ill; her registrar was away. All patients were cared for by Blythe over that period. It was only a few days.'

Joe sighed. 'Unfortunate. What do you know about him?'

She ticked off on her fingers. 'He was William Parry's predecessor, he was against William's appointment, and he wielded the fastest scalpel in the West.'

Joe's lips quirked into a smile. 'That about sums it up, from what I can gather. Everybody hated him. He hardly ever lost a baby, but he had the highest incidence of episiotomy, forceps delivery and Caesarean the hospital has ever seen.' He shrugged. 'That being the case, you might be right that the decision to operate was over-hasty. Still, there are a number of factors to consider in suggesting a trial of labour after a previous Caesarean. Have you considered them?'

'I think so.'

He twiddled a pen and leant back in his chair. 'What are they?'

'The number of previous births, the normality of any vaginal deliveries, the reason for the section, the integrity of the scar tissue, any reported abnormalities of the uterus visible on scan, the type of incision—do you want me to go on?'

He smiled slightly. 'Let's start at the top. She's had two babies, both normal and healthy, the first labour was a normal vaginal delivery but a bit slow to progress. Right?'

'Right. The second started the same way, quick-draw McGraw got wind of it and insisted she had a Caesarean—'

'You surmise.'

'I surmise. The scar looks healthy, it was a transverse lower-segment incision, and so the safest and least likely to rupture in a trial of labour, and the scan reported nothing abnormal.'

Joe stood up. 'OK. We'll go with your idea.'

'She thinks she's having a section.'

'Is that what she wants?'

Thea shook her head. 'No. I don't think so.'

'Then let's find out.'

Joe led the way back into the examination room and greeted the woman with his usual smile and handshake.

'Now, Mrs Graham, I gather you're expecting another Caesarean section. Is that right?'

She nodded. 'The doctor I saw last time told me I'd probably have one, and my GP agreed it would be safest.'

'How do you feel about that?'

'Awful. I felt really ill after the last one, whereas after the first I felt marvellous. I really enjoyed my first baby, but the second was like a stranger's baby for ages. I was so groggy.'

Joe glanced at the notes. 'I see you had a general anaesthetic. How would you feel about an epidural instead?'

She shuddered. 'Oh, no. I couldn't bear the thought of that great needle in my back. I'd have to be out cold.'

'How would you feel about having a go at a normal delivery?' he offered quietly.

'Normal—you mean like the first? Wonderful, but I didn't think I could.'

'If everything else is OK, and it seems to be, it would be possible to have what's known as a trial of labour. That means we have a theatre on standby, and we let you try and see how you get on.'

'But I fizzled out last time. I just couldn't push. My cervix dilated and nothing happened. They gave me drugs and still nothing happened, and I walked around—nothing.'

Joe looked at Thea. 'Dr Stow here feels you ought to have another chance, and I think on balance she's probably right. If you reached the same point again and we couldn't get you moving, we could always just take you to Theatre.'

She looked doubtful. 'It means going through all of that pain and the operation as well. I thought at least I'd only have the operation this time.'

Joe nodded. 'OK. We'll talk to the midwife, we'll let you go into labour naturally, but then I'd like you to come in as soon as you start having contractions and we'll have another chat, reassess and go from there. If you really don't want to give it a go when the time comes, we'll take you to Theatre. All right?'

She nodded. 'Yes. Thank you, Doctor.'

They went out and Joe shot Thea a wry look. 'They don't always want to be saved,' he said softly. He indicated the next patients. 'You take that one, I'll take this one and then we'll go for some lunch while the going's good.'

Their lunch was interrupted, however, by a little flurry of excitement. The patient who was expecting triplets had gone into labour, and there was a big sticker on her notes saying, 'GET ME STAT. JA.'

So the ward got him, and Thea by default, and on the way up he told her a little of the history.

'First pregnancy, no history, this multiple birth is a complete surprise to them and their families. Mum wants a normal delivery, Dad wants to be anywhere else in the world and admits he'll probably faint or run away, and they're both dreading the next twenty or so years. Apart from that, they're just your average couple!'

The 'average couple' and their pregnancy were being looked after in a single room on the ward when Joe and Thea arrived. Jenny greeted them with a smile. 'I've put them in here—it's nice and sunny, it's near the delivery room and it's got good access to Theatre. I take it you want blood for cross-matching, just in case?'

Joe grinned. 'Please. And a cup of coffee would be nice—we had to leave ours.'

'Ah, shame,' Jenny teased. 'Go and soothe the husband. He's petrified.'

'If I was having triplets I'd be petrified,' Joe said with a chuckle. 'Poor man. His life will never be the same again.'

'Will she be able to have a normal delivery, or are you intending to go for surgery anyway?' Thea asked.

Joe shrugged. 'We'll play it by ear. She'll have to be monitored, but the main danger is with prolapsing cords or early placental detachment. The radiologist thinks there's a singleton and a pair of identical twins, so, depending on the order they emerge in and the muddle they get the cords in, we might be lucky—and then again we might not. We'll have to suck it and see.'

'What's the main danger?'

'Apart from delivery itself? Their prematurity. The pregnancy isn't as far advanced as I would have liked, and I'd hate to lose any of them for that reason, but we can only do so much. SCBU will be standing by to receive them and we'll have a paediatrician in the room when they're born, ready to take immediate action.'

Thea nodded. That was what she had expected him to say. She must be learning! They went first and checked on the woman. Joe examined her and looked at her notes to see what the midwife had already found, and then, happy that things were proceeding quietly without drama, he and Thea went out, had the cup of coffee Jenny had made them and went up to Theatre to scrub.

'Just to be on the safe side. We don't want to waste vital time later.'

In the event there wasn't enough time to do anything. They went back in to check her, and Bev Linari was just completing an internal.

'Hi, there,' she said with a grin. 'Things are moving fast here—hope you've got your wellies on. There's lots of fluid going to be coming out in a minute.'

They laughed, and then Bev's face lost its sparkle.

'Damn monitor—it's on the blink again,' she muttered, and fiddled with the leads.

Joe stared hard at the screen and shook his head. 'I don't think so—not this time. How many centimetres dilated is she?'

'About seven, but the babes are only tiny. She's probably as good as there.'

His eyes flicked back to the screen, and he pulled on a pair of gloves and peeled back the sheet. 'Sorry to do this to you again, Mrs Gooch, but I just want to check something. One of the babies seems to be struggling a bit.'

His face went deadpan with concentration as his fingers worked, searching for clues, Thea guessed, and then as the woman gasped and he muttered an apology the trace picked up and the monitor stopped beeping.

'Cord was trying to prolapse. I pushed it back as far as I could, but when those membranes go it'll come down again. I think we ought to alert Theatre.'

Just then there was a rushing noise, and Joe jumped back as a gush of fluid poured over the edge of the bed.

The monitor went mad, Mrs Gooch groaned with the change in pressure and Joe immediately leapt forward again. 'Damn—the cord's down and the first baby's on the way fast. Mrs Gooch, you're going to have to work very hard for me for a minute, because I need to get this baby out of the way quickly.'

It came down like a rocket, Thea thought, and then stopped, just as the head was almost delivered. With a muttered apology to Mrs Gooch he picked up the episiotomy scissors and cut her tight perineum without so much as a local anaesthetic. 'Right, push,' he ordered.

Still gasping with pain and shock, she pushed and the baby advanced, only to stop again.

'Cord,' Joe and Bev both said together. Bev slipped her fingers in and searched for the cord, then, finding it, she tried to slide it over the baby's shoulder and head. 'No, it's too tight.' The monitor went crazy again. 'It must be caught on one of the other cords,' Bev said. 'You'll have to cut it; it could be tangled indefinitely.'

'Whose is it?' Joe asked.

Bev shrugged. 'Who can tell? It has to go; it's the only way forward.'

Joe swore under his breath and held out a hand. 'Clamps, please.'

He wriggled the cord out, clamped it at both ends and cut it, then all but pulled the baby clear.

The cord was intact. The cord he had cut was that of one of the other babies, and it was now without oxygen. 'Push,' he instructed. 'Just push, as hard as you can. The next one's on the way.'

Mrs Gooch tried, her husband holding her up and with a massive effort she brought the baby far enough down for Joe to slip the forceps over its head and lift it out with indecent haste.

Its cries joined those of the other baby, but it, too, had an intact cord. Bev dealt with it silently, her face grim.

Joe and Thea exchanged glances, and he turned back to the woman. 'And again, my love. One last, really big effort.'

The monitor was still emitting its warning beep, but there was a trace of a heartbeat—very fast, too fast, but there. With a superhuman effort and the benefit of a contraction, Mrs Gooch pushed down with all her strength and a very tiny baby slithered into Joe's waiting hands.

It was blue-black, lifelessly still, and Joe's face was tortured.

'Come on, little one. Let's be having you,' he said gently, and flicked the soles of its feet hard. Nothing. Not a whimper.

'Where the hell is the paediatrician?' he demanded. A nurse slipped out, and Joe grasped the baby by the ankles, and swung it through the air. 'Come on, come on— breathe, damn you!'

He laid it down, put his mouth over its face and very gently breathed out, then pushed oh, so carefully in the middle of its chest. There was a little cough, a hiccup, and then the baby drew in a lungful of air and cried.

It was only weak, a pathetic little cry, but it was a cry nonetheless. The baby was alive.

Thea felt her eyes fill but here wasn't time for sentiment. The door opened and a tall man strode in, a man she had only seen briefly from time to time. He was Andrew Barrett's SR, and he had a nurse with him.

Joe turned his head, his hands still on the mewling baby. 'Hi, Josh. One for you—slow to respond, no vital signs, I've got it going with CPR. Third born of triplets, thirty-four weeks' gestation, cord was cut because of a tangle with the first. Approximate delay from cutting the cord to the first breath was about four minutes. Can you take over?'

'Sure.' The baby disappeared into the man's big hands, lifted from the delivery table to the treatment table waiting under a heat lamp. It was still crying, its weaker cry almost drowned out by the yells of its older siblings, but it was the sweetest sound Thea had ever heard.

She wondered if Joe had got it going in time, or if the interval between cutting the cord and the first breath had been too long and the baby had sustained brain damage as a result. Had it really only been four minutes?

He was talking to the mother now, holding her hands, reassuring her. 'I'm just so sorry I had to cut you without a local, but there was no time.'

'It's all right, I understand. How are they? What are they?'

'Alive,' Joe said with a smile. 'They're alive. I'll find out.'

He turned to Thea. 'Any idea?'

'Two boys and a girl. The last one's the girl. The boys are both fine; Dr Lancaster's working on the girl.'

Josh looked up from the baby and threw them a grin. 'Seems well enough. She's much smaller than the others, but I think she's a tough little cookie. We'll get them into special care in an incubator, and you can come up and see them just as soon as you're all finished down here.'

Thea turned back towards the group, and then everything seemed to happen at once. Mrs Gooch pushed gently, a placenta slithered out onto the delivery bed and Mr Gooch rolled up his eyes and slithered quietly to the floor.

Joe lifted his head and winked at Thea. 'Oops. We've just lost your husband for a minute, Mrs Gooch. Thea, would you be kind enough to look after him? I think it's all been a bit too much.'

Thea quite agreed!

CHAPTER EIGHT

'ARE you all right?'

Joe lifted his head and met Thea's searching gaze, and she could see guilt and worry written ten feet high in the blue-grey depths of his eyes.

'We nearly lost her, Thea. It would have been my fault. I should have taken Mrs Gooch straight into Theatre and not messed about trying to give her a normal delivery.'

'Joe, there wasn't time. She progressed with astonishing speed. Her cervix just opened.'

He sighed, ramming his hands through the tangle of ash-brown hair that was the victim of his repeated attacks. 'I should have known it might. I should have moved faster.'

Thea shook her head. 'Joe, you did the only thing you could with the circumstances as they were. You had to let her deliver vaginally; you had to cut that cord. You had no choice. There were no options. Even I know that.'

He lifted his head tiredly. 'And if the baby had died?'

Thea looked down at MJ on her lap and her heart ached. 'Tragedies happen, Joe. Every day it's happening to someone.'

'But not to my patients!'

'It didn't! The baby's fine. You got them all out so fast even Bev Linari was stunned. She's never seen babies born so quickly.'

He snorted. 'Didn't have a lot of choice, did I? The first one put the wind up me. By the time the second was delivered with an intact cord I was ready to pass out like old man Gooch. I tell you, I nearly joined him on the floor when it was all over, just with sheer relief!'

He lifted the glass to his lips and took a hefty swig. Thea frowned. She'd never seen him drink spirits before, and tonight he was hitting the whisky big time.

'You'll have a hangover,' she told him.

'I don't bloody well care,' he said bluntly. He held up his finger and thumb a fraction apart. 'I came that close to losing that little one today, and I feel I've earned a damn good hangover.' He tipped the glass up again and Thea sighed.

'I'm a big boy now, Thea,' he growled. 'I can make my own decisions.'

'Of course you can.' She stood up, MJ in her arms, and headed for the door.

'Where are you going?'

'Bed. Any objections?'

'Yes. Plenty. Stay and talk.'

'Only if you stop drinking.'

He snorted. 'That's blackmail, Thea.'

'Goodnight.'

Her foot was on the bottom step when his voice reached her. 'All right, all right, I'll stop!'

She came back down. 'I'll put the baby to bed. How about coffee?'

'Was that a hint or an offer?'

She smiled. 'A hint.'

He grumbled to his feet. 'She nags and bullies me, MJ—you wait. Just now she's all sweetness and light, but you mark my words, little man. Give it ten years and you'll be running to me to save you.'

The baby ignored him. So did Thea, turning away to hide the smile on her face. 'Just make the coffee, Armitage.'

She put MJ down in his cot and went back into the sitting room to find the cat installed in her chair. 'Hey, Sylvester! That's my place.'

'Sit here with me,' Joe suggested, coming in behind her with the tray. 'That way we can share the chocolate biscuits, and I can steal a hug.'

She turned to look at him in surprise. 'Do you need a hug?' she asked.

His smile was a little off-centre. 'I was terrified, Thea. I thought I'd blown it. Of course I need a hug. Who wouldn't?'

'Oh, Joe. . .'

She took the tray and set it down, sat on the sofa and patted the cushion beside her. 'One hug coming up,' she said softly.

He lowered himself to the cushion, stretched out his legs and held out his arms.

'I thought I was hugging you?' she teased.

'Same difference. Come here and stop being right.'

She stifled the smile and moved into his arms, and then instantly realised her mistake. It just felt so incredibly right, so absolutely normal and the way it ought to be, instead of the way it could never be.

His arms closed round her, his hand cupping the back of her head, and he pulled it down onto his shoulder with a sigh. After a moment she relaxed against him. Why fight? What good would it do?

He smelled of hospitals and hibitane and soap and Joe, and she breathed in his essence surreptitiously and let herself fantasise, just for a moment. . .

'I wonder what's on telly?' he rumbled under her ear. She felt his chest shift as he reached for the remote control, then he flicked through the channels. 'There's a film starting in a minute. Want to watch it? There's nothing else.'

They watched it, Thea snuggled under Joe's arm, her head against his ribs, and after a few minutes she realised that the movie, too, was a mistake. It was quite late, well after the nine o'clock cut-off point, and the film was tasteful but occasionally sexually explicit. The hero reminded Thea a little of Joe, which did nothing for her peace of mind, and as the film progressed she realised that not only was she getting uncomfortably hot under the collar but so was he.

He had drawn one leg up to disguise the fact that he was aroused, but not before she had already realised, both from the visual evidence and the speeding beat of his heart beneath her ear.

At one point he groaned, very softly, and she almost whimpered with need. She stopped herself just in time, though, because there was one thing she had to keep remembering. She was aroused because the hero was like Joe, she was lying against Joe, and if she could have swapped them for the hero and heroine of the film she would have done so in an instant. Joe, on the other hand, was busy being turned on by the beautiful and very sexy heroine, and his reaction had nothing whatever to do with Thea's proximity.

In the end she couldn't bear it any more.

She slipped out from under his arm and wriggled to
the edge of the sofa. 'I'm going to bed,' she said in a
more or less normal voice. 'It's all right for some, but I
have to wake up in the night and I can't say I'm gripped
by the plot.'

And she all but fled out of the room. MJ was fast
asleep when she checked him, and she quickly washed,
changed into her nightshirt and slid into bed. She didn't
sleep, though. Her thoughts were too tangled, her emotions running too high, her body drawn like a bowstring
by the film.

She wanted Joe. She needed Joe.

And Joe was downstairs, oblivious to her, riveted to
the naked and beautiful woman on the screen—damn
her eyes.

Thea sighed heavily and turned her face into the pillow. She could still feel the hard solidity of his body
next to hers, could still hear the beat of his heart and
the softly muffled groan he had emitted during that one
particularly passionate scene.

If only she could make him groan like that!

It seemed like hours before he came to bed, his footsteps light on the landing, hesitating for a moment outside
her door. He said, 'Goodnight, Tink,' very softly, and if
she hadn't been so busy dreaming up fantasies with him
in the starring role she knew she wouldn't have heard
that wistful note of yearning in his voice. . .

The following morning he was gone long before she was
up and about. She had bought herself a car with her first
salary—nothing fantastic, just an elderly runabout that
would give her some independence from Joe, and him

from her—and so she loaded MJ and his kit into it and set off on her own.

She arrived on the ward to find that he had been there since six dealing with a difficult delivery that his registrar had felt needed his input. Thea's arrival coincided with the baby's, safe and well, and Joe's relief was palpable.

He and the rest of the delivery team celebrated in the ward kitchen with a cup of tea and some toast, and it was left to Thea to repair the damaged perineum. She did so quite happily, having managed several tricky repairs since she had started working under Joe, and as she carefully drew the damaged muscle layers together and sutured the tear it was satisfying to know the woman would have no trouble as a result of her poor workmanship. She had been well taught, scrupulously supervised and took a great deal of pride in her work.

Even so, when Joe came in and looked at what she had done and praised it, she felt herself glow with his words. Why it should be so important that Joe was pleased with her she didn't know. It was more than a matter of professional pride, though; she felt that if she couldn't have his interest in her personally then she'd damn well have his approval at work.

Later that morning he sprang a surprise on her. 'How do you fancy doing some gynae work today?' he asked.

'Gynae? I thought you wanted me to stick to obstetrics.'

He shrugged. 'A good GP ought to know a lot about gynaecology as well as obstetrics. I'm in Theatre this morning—why not come in and see what happens there? Just for a change. There's a woman who had a spontaneous abortion at twelve weeks who came in overnight—she'll need a scrape—and I've got a prolapse repair which could be quite interesting, and there's a woman who delivered last night at home who has a horrendous third-degree tear which needs dealing with under GA. It should be quite tricky—we'll tackle that one first.'

'What if someone needs help in the meantime?'

'Then you can come out. Don't worry about it. Come for a while, anyway.'

She did, and was horrified at the tear the first patient had suffered. The baby was an afterthought born fifteen years after her last child, her tissues had lost their elasticity and it would take all Joe's skill and ingenuity to get her back to anything approaching normal. The only consolation was that having the baby in the hospital wouldn't have affected the outcome in this respect, so the woman didn't need to reproach herself.

Thea perched on a stool behind and to the right of Joe, and watched, fascinated, as he carefully and meticulously drew the ripped tissues together. And she thought she'd done well with her repair earlier!

She suddenly realised just how much she had to learn.

By the end of the morning Thea decided that she preferred obstetrics to gynaecology. OK, the gynae was very interesting and technically challenging, but obstetrics had the wonderful reward of new life, and for Thea that made all the difference.

She said so to Joe as they sat over coffee that night, and he smiled ruefully. 'You too? I feel just the same. I do the gynae because it's a part of the job, and I do it well because I feel it's important to do everything as well as I can, but the obs I do for love.'

She grinned. 'Does that mean I don't get a bill from you for delivering MJ?'

His face changed, almost imperceptibly. 'I charge double for candlelight deliveries,' he told her, and despite the teasing tone of his voice she had a feeling he was disturbed at her bringing the subject up.

Why? Was it that embarrassment again? Why was it only with her that he was embarrassed? Because he regarded her as a sister? Probably. She gave up trying to work it out, her mind moving on to something that had been worrying her.

She was chewing her lip, mulling over the problem when Joe spoke. 'What is it, Tink?'

She looked up, startled, to find his eyes on her, searching her face. 'I was thinking about MJ.'

'What about him?'

'I haven't made that will yet.'

'Take tomorrow off,' Joe insisted. 'Go and see a solicitor and get it fixed. It's so easy to put off things like that.'

She toyed with her coffee for a moment, then nodded. 'OK, I will. Do you have a solicitor I can use?'

Joe nodded. 'I use a firm in town. They've got people who specialise. I saw a woman about my will— Mrs Avery.'

'You've got a will?'

'Of course.'

'Oh!' Thea twinkled at him. 'Do I get a mention?'

'Yes,' Joe said drily. 'I'm leaving you my stamp collection.'

Her brows quirked together. 'You haven't got a stamp collection.'

'Well, silly me,' he murmured. 'Perhaps it was my pressed flowers?'

Thea scowled. 'You aren't going to tell me, are you?'

He leant over and tweaked her nose. 'No, Tink, I'm not, so you can stop trying to wheedle it out of me. Anyway, if I have any say in it it'll be irrelevant for a good forty years at least, so I shouldn't hold your breath.'

She laughed. 'All right, I won't, and I'll ring up and make an appointment in the morning, but they may not be able to see me just like that.'

'Try, anyway. Take the time off whenever it suits them—we'll sort out cover.'

In the event they could fit her in, and so she went down at ten from the hospital, sorted out the details very quickly with Joe's Mrs Avery and was back on the ward before eleven.

'Go down to the crèche—MJ needs a feed,' Joe told her when she arrived back.

'But I've been out almost all morning—'

'Just do it quickly. I need your help in Theatre in half an hour.'

She went, feeding the baby in record time, and was back in Theatre twenty-five minutes later to find the patient on the table and Joe about to start.

'Ah, Thea. Great. Come and see—I'm doing a hysterectomy for fibroids, and on scan they looked vast. I think it could be quite impressive.'

It was. Thea was amazed that the woman's abdomen could contain such a heavy mass of fibroids without her bleeding to death or being thought permanently pregnant. The difference in the size of her abdomen when Joe closed the incision was clearly noticeable, and he remarked on it with characteristic bluntness.

'Well, she'll be pleased,' he said. 'Quickest way I know to lose two stone.'

'Never mind feeling better,' Thea added.

'Oh, she'll certainly do that. She's been feeling terrible for ages but thought it was the change. It seems she'd had a whole string of symptoms—heavy periods, pain on intercourse, bleeding after intercourse, dragging sensation, bowel disturbances, bladder problems due to the pressure, extreme tiredness and loss of energy—the list was endless. She finally went to the GP to go on HRT to settle some of her ''little difficulties''. Judging by the mess we found, I think the GP picked it up in the nick of time.'

The fibrotic uterus, looking like nothing so much as an enormous bunch of red grapes, was sent off to the lab for examination to make sure that there was nothing insidious contained in its mass, and Joe and Thea went to grab lunch before going back to the ward, Thea for routine ward work, Joe to get on top of some of his paperwork.

She went into his office at five, just as she was knocking off, and found him deep in dictating letters. 'Shall I just go on home?' she asked.

He nodded. 'Yes. I'll finish off here and make my way back later—want me to pick up a take-away?'

Thea sighed. 'I was supposed to be cooking and housekeeping for you in return for my keep,' she reminded him.

'That was before you were working. You can't juggle a home, a young baby and a job, Thea.'

'Then I should pay you.'

His reply was rude and to the point, and left her in no
doubt about his feelings.

'I'm not sure that's anatomically possible,' she
told him.

He growled, and she threw up her hands. 'Fine,' she
said with a grin. 'Pick up a take-away. I'll go home and
put my feet up.'

'You do that—you look shattered.'

She went, feeling even more tired after that remark,
and fell asleep in the middle of feeding MJ.

Joe found her like that, slumped in the armchair, the
sleeping baby at her breast, and without waking her he
took MJ out of her arms and eased her shirt down so
that it covered her again. Then he went upstairs with the
baby, bathed him and put him down in his cot, and went
back down to find Thea still asleep.

She looked shattered. She was doing too much, there
was no doubt. He ought to talk to her—perhaps she
should give up breast-feeding now, or cut it down to one
feed a day, perhaps the morning feed. There was research
which showed a significant increase in energy levels in
women who stopped breast-feeding at around this time,
and Thea could certainly do with an increase in energy.

She was killing herself, the silly kid, and it was his
fault. He shouldn't have offered her the job, but if he
hadn't she'd be working somewhere else by now, he was
sure, and working far harder because he wouldn't be
around to take up the slack. As it was, he was having to
burn the candle at both ends a bit, but he didn't mind—
not for Thea.

It was the least he could do, and he'd do it willingly,

but to be fair to her she ought to have a normal workload. He didn't believe in cheating people or allowing them to win. Pride came from knowing that the job was done well, and it was no good if it was only half the job.

He'd bring up the subject of MJ's feeding and routine later, when she was awake, but for now he'd put the take-away in the oven and let her sleep.

'Give up? But why?'

'To give you more energy.'

Thea pushed her hair back absently and searched his face for any hidden messages. 'I'm not pulling my weight, am I?'

He looked away, a sure sign that she was right. 'We aren't talking about your job now—'

'I'm not, am I? Pulling my weight? I should be doing nights, and working late, and instead it's you doing it. That's not fair, Joe. You've finished with that. You're a consultant. That means your juniors consult you on matters too complex for them. You should be a trainer, a demonstrator, a troubleshooter, not a houseman in your spare time!'

His mouth quirked in a grin. 'There are those who would say at least I'm earning my money at the moment.'

She borrowed his earlier comment, and he arched a brow. 'I'm not sure it's anatomically possible,' he said mildly.

She threw a cushion at him. 'Take a hike,' she said. 'You're spoiling me, Joe, and it isn't fair on me, or you, or the rest of your staff. I want the proper workload, or not at all.'

'Then you'll need to wean MJ,' he said seriously.

'He's four and a half months old now. He'll be fine. He's having solids already.'

Thea knew he was right. 'I'll start at the weekend,' she promised. 'Then next week I can start doing the job I'm being paid for.'

'OK,' Joe agreed quietly, 'but keep him on one or two feeds, just for a while. Don't drop everything.'

'I'll see.'

She did see. She saw that she felt much better without the extra day feeds and expressing MJ's top-up feeds, and she also saw just how much Joe must have been covering for her. Even now she couldn't have done the job without his help, because if she was on overnight it was Joe who did the babyminding.

She seemed to be a permanent drain on him, one way or the other, and she felt racked with guilt, but it was too bad. There was only another month left to go and she would be moving on. She'd better look for another job.

In the meantime she had this one to do, and do it she would.

The first night she spent in the hospital on duty seemed endless. Although she had been getting up in the night to MJ, she had forgotten how it felt to be up all night, to doze off and be called out of bed again, and again, and again. Every time she got up she had to drag her eyes open and sluice her face in cold water to try and wake up. Unfortunately she couldn't sluice her mind with cold water or she would have done.

She knew she couldn't have done this after she'd gone back to work—not without a full-time nanny or au pair, and certainly not while breast-feeding. Without Joe it wouldn't have been possible for her to do the job, and indeed, without Joe it still wouldn't be possible.

She coped quite well. She had been taught how to use the ventouse, and during her first night she was called to a woman who had simply run out of steam right at the end. She had been labouring hard all day and Thea had been sure she would end up helping her, so it was no surprise when the call came.

She dragged her coat on over her rumpled clothes, scraped her hair back into a pony-tail to contain it and splashed her face, then made her way onto the ward.

It was hushed and peaceful, with only the distant crying of a single baby to disturb the quiet night. Thea went into the delivery room and found the midwife, Sue, still encouraging the tired mother.

She was lying on her side, too exhausted to sit up or kneel, and Thea went up to her and took her hand.

'Hello, Debbie. Having trouble finding the energy?'

Debbie nodded. 'I'm just so tired,' she whispered, and she sounded on the verge of tears.

'Let's see if we can give you a hand.'

Thea scrubbed her hands, pulled on gloves, examined the woman, and found that the baby was almost right down. The hair was just visible, and if she was lucky she'd be able to get the suction cup positioned.

She squeezed the soft silicone cup closed a little, edged it in towards the back of the baby's head and let it go. Then she turned on the suction a little and tested to see if she had a good grip.

No. Blast. She tried again, and again, and finally the third time the cup held. Turning up the suction to give a nice powerful grip, she waited for a contraction, then with Sue's help and encouragement to guide Debbie, they worked together to bring the baby down.

It did progress, thankfully. There was no reason why it shouldn't, or none that Thea had detected, but that didn't necessarily mean anything.

'All right, one more good push,' she said encouragingly as Debbie groaned again, and this time the baby came right down and crowned. The next push would deliver the head.

'Do you think I should do an episiotomy?' Thea asked Sue quietly.

Sue examined the taut perineum and shrugged her shoulders slightly. 'Maybe. I don't think she'll do it intact, but she might only have a little tear. Just ease gently; let her do most of it. Now the head's down against the perineum her own expulsions will pick up—that might be enough.'

So Thea waited, using the cup to guide as much as anything, and as the woman began to pant Sue indicated that she should pull the head gently forwards, to lift it over the rim of the perineum.

Then inch by inch the baby's face appeared, and seconds later the shoulders, first one, then the other, and the baby slipped out with a splosh into Sue's hands.

Thea, unable to contain her smile, turned off the ventouse machine, disconnected the cup and winked at Sue.

'Piece of cake,' she murmured.

'Of course.'

They swapped grins, checked the baby and the time, and handed her to her exhausted mother. Tears trickled down Debbie's cheeks. 'Oh, little one, I thought you were never coming out,' she said softly.

Thea blinked to clear her suddenly blurred vision, smiled apologetically at Sue and then checked Debbie's perineum.

'Little graze. I think it could be left—what do you think?'

Sue agreed. 'Well done. I'm glad you didn't give her an episiotomy. That'll heal before you would have finished stitching a cut.'

Thea chuckled. 'So skilful,' she said with a shrug, and patted Debbie on the arm. 'Well done. I'll leave you with Sue now. You'll be fine.'

And she went back to bed to try and sleep.

The next call was to A and E, for a woman with heavy bleeding in early pregnancy following a minor car accident. She had apparently already been spotting on and off for a few days, and the shock had just pushed her over the edge.

Feeling that it was probably for the best if the pregnancy had already gone wrong, Thea admitted her for a scan and probable D and C in the morning, and went back to bed.

Another patient on gynae was in acute post-operative pain and needed an injection at three a.m., and then just as she was dozing off again at four she was called to assist at another labour.

This one was beyond her range of experience and she had no choice but to call the SR.

He came, took the woman to Theatre and delivered the baby by Caesarean section with Thea assisting. Being a gentleman, he left her to close and went back to his bed, and so it was six-thirty before she was finished.

It hardly seemed worth bothering about bed again, so

she showered and changed and went down to the canteen for breakfast. She found Gavin Jones there, looking equally bleary-eyed, and went and joined him.

'Hi. How's the baby?' she asked, summoning a weary smile.

'Lovely. She will have grown again by the time I get to see her next. I haven't been home since yesterday morning.'

'I know the feeling. I saw my baby last night for about an hour before he went home with Joe. I don't suppose he'll recognise me by lunchtime.'

Gavin gave a short grunt of laughter. 'Hell, isn't it? Why do we do it?'

'Well, it isn't the pay—not yet, at least—so it must be love.'

Gavin snorted again. 'Oh, yeah. Sure. I love spending all night in Theatre failing to save a patient who's chucked himself through a plate-glass window in a ram-raid.'

'Ow. Well, at least you didn't have to feel too sorry for him.'

Gavin looked at her wryly. 'No? He was seventeen. I've just finished talking to his parents.'

'Oh, dear.'

'Yes, "oh, dear" indeed. Oh, well, I'm not God. You do what you can, and what you can't you have to accept.'

'It can be difficult, though.'

'Impossible sometimes,' Gavin said quietly. 'I wonder if when the general public complain about our lack of communication skills they have any idea what we might have just been dealing with, and how hard it can be to just dismiss it and move on?' He sighed, pushed back his chair and stretched out his long legs. 'How are you getting on with Obs and Gobs?'

She smiled at his terminology. 'OK. I love the babies.'

Gavin chuckled tiredly and closed his eyes. 'We all love the babies. Are you going to specialise?'

Thea shook her head. 'No. I'm going into general practice.'

He cracked an eye open. 'Really? You must be nuts. You want to stay in hospital medicine, get a consultancy and go for a nice steady nine to five.'

She laughed. 'What, like Joe?'

'Mostly it's all right.'

'But you have to get there first. No, I like the idea of being a GP, and it can fit in well with being a mother. You have to remember I'm a single parent.'

Gavin pushed himself up the chair again and studied her thoughtfully. 'It must be very hard.'

She smiled wistfully. 'It can be. Joe's been wonderful. I couldn't have done it without him.'

'No. He's very generous with his time and friendship, isn't he? I've never heard anybody grumble about him, ever, and in this place that has to be a record.'

He pushed himself to his feet and grinned. 'Back to the treadmill. See you, Thea.'

She watched him go, his words echoing in her head. Yes, she thought, he was generous with his time and friendship. Very generous. More generous than she had any right to expect or demand.

She would start looking for a placement as a GP trainee now, before their friendship was strained beyond endurance.

CHAPTER NINE

'You look shattered.'

'I am shattered.'

Joe put his hands on Thea's shoulders and pushed her gently towards the stairs. 'Go to bed.'

'I have to deal with the baby.'

'I'll deal with the baby.'

'But I should—'

'You should stop arguing and do as you're told. You're exhausted. You're not going to be any good to anyone in your current state, least of all the baby. Now hop it.'

She went, dragging herself up the stairs with her last dregs of energy. 'Wake me at nine. I'll feed him.'

'I'll think about it.'

She stopped and turned back, looking down at him in the hall. 'Joe, I won't go to bed if you don't promise.'

He sighed. 'All right, I'll wake you at nine.'

She went then, too tired to think any more. She was asleep before her head hit the pillow, and when Joe came in at nine she was less than polite.

'It was your idea, Tink,' he reminded her as he went back downstairs.

'Kind of you to point that out,' she grumbled.

She swung her legs over the edge of the bed and stumbled across the room to the bathroom. A quick wash and she woke up a little, enough to negotiate the stairs in reasonable safety at least.

150

Joe was in the kitchen with MJ, who was balanced on his arm, pulling Joe's hair and laughing.

'Ouch. That hurts, little man. Put me down—ow! Steady, son, a game's a game but that's enough.' He prised off the tiny fingers, picked the bits of soggy rusk out of his hair and then turned to see Thea in the doorway.

'Um—hi. He's bright as a button.'

'So I see,' she said drily. 'I'm glad one of us is.'

She sat at the table and held out her arms, and Joe put the gurgling baby on her knee. He gripped her sleeves and started to bounce on her lap. 'Gymnastics now, is it? Just use me as a trampoline, my darling. Who cares about the bruises, eh? Who cares?'

She snuggled him in her arms, loving the feel of his little body, but he protested and pushed away, bouncing again and laughing at her.

'Pest. Do you want feeding?'

'I gave him a rusk,' Joe told her.

She looked at his mucky little face. 'So I see. I think, to be honest, he just wants to play at the moment. I could have stayed asleep, nuisance,' she said lovingly.

'It was your idea,' Joe reminded her again. 'Why don't you go in the sitting room and I'll bring you a cup of tea?'

'I'd rather have a glass of wine.'

'You can have that afterwards. Go on, do as you're told.'

She went, the baby perched on her hip, and turned the cat off her chair so she could sit down. She put MJ down on the floor on his playmat so he could practise rolling over, and watched him with glazed eyes as she sipped the tea Joe brought her. 'Lovely,' she murmured. 'You were right—I needed tea.'

Joe, sprawled on the sofa with the cat, grinned. 'Of course. I'm always right.'

She poked her tongue out, leant back and closed her eyes. 'Are nights always that long?' she asked, her voice slurred with relaxation.

'Only when you're working. When you're off duty they're over in a flash.'

She chuckled. 'How true. I wonder when that baby will feel like having a feed and going to bed?'

'He looks wide awake to me.'

'That's what I thought. Depressing, isn't it?'

But by the time she'd finished her tea he was beginning to grizzle, and she picked him up and looked at Joe. 'Mind if I feed him here?'

'Of course not,' he said. He sounded surprised that the question would occur to her, but she had been avoiding feeding MJ in Joe's presence for some time and it seemed odd now that he was there.

Still, she couldn't be bothered to move yet, and it was nothing he hadn't seen before. She pulled her T-shirt up, unclipped her bra and MJ latched on without fuss, snuggling closer as she held him. She missed feeding him during the day and was so glad she'd kept this one feed going. Now, though, for some reason MJ seemed restless.

He pulled away and cried, and she looked at him, perplexed. 'What is it, little one? Want to try the other side first?'

She swapped him round, but within moments he was grizzling again, as if he was still hungry. She looked at her breast and noticed for the first time that it seemed softer, empty.

Tears filled her eyes. 'Oh, no,' she whispered.

Joe was beside her immediately. 'What is it, sweetheart?'

'I haven't got any milk to give him. Oh Joe. . .' And she closed her eyes, spilling the hot, fat tears down over her cheeks to splash on her empty breasts.

'Shh, Thea, don't fret. I'll make him a bottle. I expect you're just overtired and dehydrated. I'll get you some more tea in a moment, after I've made the feed. Hang on, love.'

He rumpled her hair and went out, leaving her face to face with the reality of juggling a baby and a job. Of course it wouldn't do MJ any harm to be bottle-fed from now. Most women only breast-fed for a short while. It was just that she had been determined not to wean him yet and now her body seemed to be giving her no choice.

More tears sipped silently down her cheeks, and Joe came back and handed her the bottle, wiping the tears away with his thumbs and kissing her head in gentle encouragement.

'Don't cry, my love,' he murmured, and it sounded so loving, so much how she had wanted him to sound that she nearly wept again. He was only being kind. She wasn't really his love at all.

She sniffed and turned her attention to the baby, holding the bottle up for him and watching as he greedily and gratefully drained it in short order. Then Joe took him, winded him without preamble and handed her another cup of tea. 'Drink it, it's cool enough; then you can have a small glass of wine to help you relax.'

He took the baby upstairs and came down again a few minutes later. Thea could hear MJ still grizzling a little in his cot and she looked up at Joe worriedly. 'Is he still hungry?'

'No, he's overtired. Thea, stop worrying. Babies do cry from time to time for no very good reason. They just get fed up, like the rest of us.' He crouched by his hi-fi system and flicked through the CDs, finally selecting one and dropping it in the drawer of the CD player.

Clannad's soft, slightly mystic music filled the room and Joe came over to her. 'Come here,' he murmured, and drew her to her feet, then led her to the sofa. He sat at one end and told her to lie down with her head on his lap. 'Your neck's all tense. You could do with a massage.'

How her neck could be tense she didn't know. She thought it sounded as if it would take far too much energy, but of course he was right. She realised it as soon as his hand cupped her nape and she felt the tension drain away with every rhythmic squeeze of his fingers.

Her eyes closed. It felt wonderful. Between the wine, the music and the gentle touch of his hand, she felt the watch-spring of her nerves and muscles give way, leaving her boneless. Her hand was draped over his thigh, just above the knee, and she could feel the corded strength of his muscles under her palm. She almost gave in to the urge to stroke her hand over his leg, to feel the muscled thigh bunch and tense at her touch, but she stopped herself just in time.

'I ought to go to bed before I fall asleep,' she murmured, and pushed herself up and away from him before she did something silly and gave her feelings away.

'Me too,' he agreed, and stood up beside her, flicking off the hi-fi with the remote control and turning off the lights. She carried her cup and glass though to the kitchen and turned to leave, to find Joe in her path. He set down his glass and put his hands on her shoulders, and as she tipped her head back to look at him he lowered his head to kiss her forehead.

His lips missed their target, settling instead on her mouth. For the merest second he hesitated, then he kissed her, the gentlest, chastest kiss, which nevertheless threatened to buckle her knees and turn her to jelly.

Then he lifted his head and brushed her cheek with his knuckles. 'Don't worry about MJ, Tink. He'll be fine. Just go to bed and rest.'

'I will. Thanks for everything, Joe,' she whispered, and, going up on tiptoe, she kissed him again, just briefly, because once hadn't been enough.

Then she turned and ran upstairs before she could do anything else. . .

'Mrs Graham's in labour. She's on her way in.'

Joe looked up from his endless paperwork and his brows knotted together in a frown. 'Mrs Graham?'

'The woman with normal but slow first labour and Caesarean birth for the second child because of failure to progress. We were going to give her a trial of labour.'

'Ah, yes.' He capped his pen and leant back. 'Want to deal with it?'

'We were going to talk to her again, see how she felt. She might be more reassured if you see her.'

'Play it by ear,' he advised. 'Clerk her on admission, chat to her, see how far she's got. Take Bev Linari's advice—is she on today?'

Thea nodded. 'Yes, she's on a late.'

'Fine. Keep me posted.'

So Thea went and clerked Mrs Graham, and found as before that she was a little apprehensive about having to go through not only a labour but an operation as well.

'If we can keep you comfortable during your labour, with gas and air and relaxation exercises, and perhaps the TENS machine, which works by giving your nerves little electric tingles and somehow confuses them so the pain doesn't register—if we can make you comfortable enough so you don't suffer, wouldn't it be worth a try? Think of how much better you'd feel afterwards if you could avoid an operation.'

Reluctantly, Mrs Graham agreed to see how it went, and after about an hour Bev bleeped Thea and she came back up from Gynae. Bev met her outside the sluice.

'You rang, milady?' Thea said with a smile.

'Yup. Mrs G. She's getting a bit more distressed, and the TENS doesn't seem to be working. I thought of suggesting the pool.'

Thea shrugged. 'You can try. She seems fairly traditional in her thinking, so she might not be willing to throw her clothes off and leap in there, and I can't imagine for a moment that she'll stay there till the end and have her husband joining her in his undies, but you never can tell.'

Bev chuckled. 'You never can. William Parry did, when his wife Charlotte had their baby—oh, a couple of years ago now, I suppose. That was quite fun.'

'William did that?' Thea said, amazed. 'What an astounding thought.' She tried to picture the good-looking consultant obstetrician in the birthing pool in his boxer shorts, and failed miserably.

'Charlotte wanted him in there, so he went.' Bev's face sobered. 'Of course, he'd lost the other one so tragically along with his wife, I think he probably felt Charlotte and the baby were a miracle. He would have done anything Charlotte asked him, I think.'

'How did his first wife die?' Thea asked quietly.

'She was shot—mugged by a youth at the cashpoint machine. They never caught him.'

Thea was shocked. 'How dreadful,' she whispered. 'Oh, Bev, how would you get over that?'

'Love, I reckon. It still hurts him, of course, but Charlotte's changed him so much. He smiles with his eyes now. He never used to.'

He did smile with his eyes. Thea had noticed that. Was that what love did to you? Joe smiled with his eyes too, but there was always something else there, a hidden sadness that never really went away. She guessed that he would always be scarred by the tragedy of his childhood. Losing your parents so suddenly in a car accident was bad enough for a twelve-year-old. The uncle and cousins had been the last straw.

She wondered what would have become of Joe if her father hadn't intervened, and decided with a shudder that it didn't bear thinking about. 'How about Mrs Graham, then?' she said to Bev, and they went back into the labour ward, where the woman was lying on her side, her husband holding her hand, breathing through a contraction with her.

When it had subsided Thea and Bev discussed the idea of the pool with her.

'Get in the water? Oh, I don't know—I've heard all sorts of strange things about it. Doesn't the baby drown?'

Bev shook her head. 'I've never lost a baby yet with an underwater birth, but we were thinking more in terms of the first stage while your cervix dilates. It can be very comforting and often speeds labour up.'

So Mrs Graham allowed herself to be talked into it, and Bev went to prepare the pool while Thea went back downstairs to her gynae lady.

She was wondering how things were going when she was bleeped again, and went back up to find Mrs Graham in the pool, very relaxed and declaring it to be the most wonderful invention.

'She's fully dilated, and she's stopped dead,' Bev told Thea quietly. 'No problem with the baby, Mrs G's quite happy, so I suggest we just wait.'

'What else can we do?'

'Operate?'

'With no evidence of distress? Have her membranes ruptured yet?'

Bev shook her head. 'When they do I'll get her out and make her walk round, because I want to check the liquor for meconium. If the baby's distressed its bowels will start working and I want to be the first to know.'

Thea nodded. 'I'll check with Joe about leaving her. I'd rather it was his decision.'

She went and found him still submerged in his office, but this time with his secretary. He was smiling at her, and Thea could see why. She was pretty, in her early twenties with a figure like a supermodel, and she fancied Joe. All this Thea knew from one glance, and she hated the girl on sight! She told herself to grow up and got to the point.

'Mrs Graham's fully dilated and ground to a halt, but

the baby's fine, she's fine and I think she should be allowed to continue for a while.'

'Membranes still intact?'

'Yes.'

'OK. I'll just finish what I'm doing with Emily and I'll come and see how it's going.'

Thea nodded and went out, closing the door very carefully. She wanted to slam it, childishly, because the sight of Emily simpering at Joe and him smiling so fondly at her made her feel sick. She marched back to the delivery room and found Bev helping Mrs Graham out of the water.

'Membranes have just gone, so I thought we could walk round,' Bev said with a smile.

Thea nodded. 'Good idea. How's the baby's heartbeat?'

'Fine—nice and steady, about one thirty-five.'

One hundred and thirty-five beats a minute was well within the normal range, and Thea was happy with that. She looked at the charts, saw that Mrs Graham was walking round well-supported by her husband and Bev, and headed for the door.

She had just gone through it when Joe came striding down the corridor. 'Lord, that girl is vapid!' he muttered. 'She'll be the death of me. I have to check everything she does for me, and it's driving me cuckoo!'

Thea felt a little spurt of satisfaction and had to quell the smile. 'Get a new one,' she suggested. 'Someone older and more experienced.'

'I may well do that,' he growled. 'Right, how's tricks with Mrs G?'

'Slow. She's all right.'

'Let's have a look at her.'

Joe went in, Thea in his wake, and he chatted for a moment to Mrs Graham and then suggested she should hop up on the bed so that he could examine her.

While she climbed awkwardly onto the bed and lay down, he washed his hands, dried them and tugged on a pair of gloves. 'OK. Let's see what's going on.'

He put one hand on her abdomen and with the other he gently explored her cervix. After a second his brows knotted together and he turned to her. 'Feel that?'

'Your hand?'

'No, the contraction.'

She shook her head. 'I'm not having a contraction.'

'You are—or you were. It's gone now. I'll just wait for another to check, but if I'm right you should be able to start pushing when you're told you've got a contraction, and then hopefully you'll make some progress. Your cervix is completely out of the way, so it's not going to hold you up— Yes, there you are. Another one. Feel it?'

She shook her head.

'Bev, you feel it.'

The midwife put her hand on Mrs Graham's abdomen, and blinked. 'Good Lord. There's a thing. It's very weak—it seems to be round the back more.'

'It is. I can feel the back of her cervix pulling up. Right, let's get you into a better position to let gravity help—how about a beanbag, Bev?'

'Fine.' The midwife disappeared and came back with a beanbag, setting it down against the wall with plenty of room around it. 'Hop off the bed, my love, and come and squat down here and we'll see if we can get some progress going here.'

In the end it was Thea who had her hand on the abdomen, feeling the contractions and cheerleading because Bev couldn't feel them and monitor the baby at the same time, Joe who was crouching between Mrs Graham's knees and pulling steadily with the ventouse and Bev, with her head to the ear trumpet, listening to the baby's heartbeat and reporting to Joe.

Mr Graham stood at arm's length, holding his wife's hand, unable to get any closer for the overcrowding, and finally, without any real drama, the baby slithered into the world in wonderful condition and announcing his displeasure for all to hear.

Joe stood up and winked at Thea. 'Good idea of mine, this trial of labour,' he murmured as they were leaving a few moments later.

'It was my idea!' she protested.

He smiled. 'I'd always intended to let her do this. I was sure we could get that baby out safely. If I'd had the slightest doubt, she would have been in Theatre. I don't take risks, not for anybody's ego.'

Thea, who'd thought she had been the real mover and shaker in the whole business, was disillusioned and cross. 'I really thought I'd changed your mind. You might have let me think that.'

He laughed. 'Isn't it better that we agreed?'

She stopped fuming and smiled at him wearily. 'I suppose so. Yes, of course it is. I'm sorry.'

'So, who's going to do the needlework?'

'Is there much?'

'A little. I was very careful.'

She smirked. 'I did a ventouse last week with no tear at all.'

'Clever clogs.'

'Of course.' They exchanged a smile, and Thea went back to the delivery room, where Bev had just finished delivering the placenta.

Thea checked it with her, marvelling over the astonishingly ingenious construction of an organ that could filter and cleanse and supply nutrients and so very, very rarely failed.

'There are lots of rituals to do with the placenta,' Bev told them. 'In some countries it's buried in certain orientations depending on whether you want the child to travel far or always return home, and sometimes it's buried under roses, but it's said to be bad luck not to bury it so deep that dogs can't get to it because if a dog eats a placenta it's said to bring bad luck to the child for life.

'So much mysticism in such ancient cultures—almost as if the vital role it plays has been understood and revered for thousands of years, and yet even now we hardly know its secrets.'

'He couldn't care less about the rituals,' Mrs Graham said with a chuckle. 'He's quite happy where he is.'

She was propped up in the delivery bed, feeding him, and Thea left them there while she washed her hands and gowned up. Then Mr Graham was handed his son to hold and Thea started the intricate needlework to repair the little tear.

To do Joe credit, the baby was bigger than the one she had delivered, and the tear was only tiny. If she felt magnanimous, she thought she might tell him so later. She hid a smile and concentrated on her job.

*   *   *

There was no time to tell Joe anything later. A woman came in with abdominal pain, and Thea admitted her and called Joe. They were due to go off duty in about an hour, and Thea had a feeling that one of them wouldn't be making it home.

'We've got a patient in, admitted by the GP. Thirty weeks' gestation, abdominal pain, nothing abnormal detected, heartbeat all right, no blood loss, cervix closed, no uterine contractions—she might just have eaten something.'

'Mmm,' Joe said, and went into the room to examine the patient.

She was married, in her early twenties, and it was her first baby. Both she and her husband were looking worried, and Thea could tell that they felt there was something wrong with the baby.

'I'd like you to have a scan,' Joe said. 'It will help us to decide what the problem is, and if it's anything to do with the baby.' He turned to Thea. 'Bleep me when we get the results, please—and you'd better contact the crèche and tell them we'll be late. I want to see this one through and I may need you. Take some blood too, please.'

She booked the scan, waited for the result and told Joe. 'Looks like an area of placental detachment. I've just checked her again and her blood pressure seems to have dropped a little. I think she might be having an antepartum haemorrhage.'

'How's the baby?'

'All right at the moment. Heartbeat was a little fast.'

'Theatre. We can't afford to mess about. Get some blood ordered—did you cross-match?'

'Yes, it's done. The blood's on its way up and there's an anaesthetist on stand-by. They're ready for us.'

'Fine. Let's go.'

They moved as fast as they could, but it wasn't fast enough. The baby was delivered five minutes later by Caesarean section, perfect in every way but one.

They had been too late.

Joe handed the baby to Thea. 'Wrap him up and take him to the father.'

She took the lifeless little body in her hands and stared down at it in disbelief. She had listened to his heartbeat, seen it on the scan. He couldn't be—

'Dead' was too final a word to use.

She wiped his face with a swab, wrapped him in a towel and carried him out of the theatre.

The man was sitting outside, his hands locked together, his head bowed.

'Mr James?'

He looked up. He already knew, Thea could tell. She held the baby out to him. 'I'm sorry. We were too late.'

He stood up slowly and moved towards her, then after an endless moment he looked down at the peaceful face of his tiny son. His eyes closed, but not before Thea saw the grief that emptied them of hope.

She put the baby in his arms and he held him as if he was the most precious thing in the world.

A nurse appeared at her side. 'Want me to take over?' she asked softly. 'Mr Armitage wants you back in there to help.'

She went back without a word, scrubbed and gowned up again, and ready to assist. She held retractors, clamped blood vessels, sucked the blood out of the uterus and watched as Joe repaired the carnage, stopped the bleeding and gave Mrs James back another chance at life and motherhood.

Then when they were done she tore off her gown and gloves, shoved open the door and ran away from the theatre as fast as her legs would carry her.

The lift was too slow, so she sprinted down the stairs, along the corridor and into the nursery.

'Where is he?' she asked Angela without preamble.

'Having a rest. What is it?'

She pushed past the woman and went into the quiet room, then lifted MJ carefully into her arms. He cried, and she soothed him automatically, rocking him to comfort him—or herself. She wasn't sure. She couldn't think. All she could see was the tiny, beautiful face of Baby James, and the grief in his father's eyes. . .

'Thea?'

She lifted her head. 'Hello, Joe,' she said woodenly.

'Time to go home, sweetheart.' His voice was gentle, his hands careful with her, as if he knew she'd shatter if he moved too fast.

They left her car at the hospital by tacit agreement, and Joe drove her home. He didn't interfere once they got there, just made her some tea while she fed the baby in silence, her eyes fixed on him as he suckled at her breast. There wasn't much milk for him any more, but it was a comfort to them both and Thea needed the ritual.

Then she changed him and put him down, still in silence. He was asleep as she laid him in the cot, and she stood there for an age, just staring at him and wondering how that young woman would cope with her terrible sadness.

Then she felt Joe's hands on her shoulders, turning her into his arms, and she realised she was crying, huge racking sobs that threatened to tear her apart.

'Why, Joe?' she whispered. 'Why?'

His hands tightened on her back, pulling her harder against him, giving her his strength. 'Who knows?' he murmured.

'Will they have a funeral?'

He dragged in a deep breath. 'Yes, I think so. They usually do.'

'Oh, God. How will they survive?'

He didn't answer. There was no answer he could have given. Instead he held her in the darkness, and she wondered at his pain. When she'd had MJ a nurse had told her that Joe took the loss of his babies personally, and Thea wondered now how he was feeling. She rubbed her hands over his back in a soothing gesture and he sighed and rested his chin against her hair.

'OK now?' he asked softly.

She sniffed. 'Mmm. Sorry.'

'Don't be. I've made more tea and done some toast for you.'

'What about you?'

'I'm not hungry.'

He moved away from her. 'Come on down when you're ready. I've got some things to see to in the study.'

She followed him down a few minutes later after she had washed her face and tucked MJ in and shed a few more tears; then as she passed his study door she felt a deep, terrible pain—not hers, but of someone close to her. Someone she loved.

She opened the door a crack. 'Joe?'

'I'm busy, Thea,' he muttered.

'In the dark?' She pushed the door wide open and went in. He was sitting in the big, high-backed chair with his back to her, and as she went round the side she saw that his face was streaked with tears.

'Oh, Joe,' she whispered. 'Don't cry alone.'

She sat on his lap and wrapped her arms around him, drawing his head down on her breasts.

A great shudder ran through him, and then his arms came round her and his shoulders heaved. 'Shh, love, I've got you,' she whispered, and she held him as the tears ran down his cheeks and soaked into her blouse, and his sobs shook her.

'Damn,' he whispered harshly. 'Why, Thea? Why does it happen? We were so close—just another minute or two—'

Another shudder went through him, and she pressed her lips to his hair. 'I don't know. I don't understand either. I just know it's terribly unfair and I'm very glad I'm not God and don't have to decide who will live and who will die.'

She stood up, moving away to the window to stand looking out into the dusk. It was July, a lovely evening, and yet in her heart it was bitter winter. 'It wasn't your fault, Joe.'

'I could have operated when she came in.'

'And you might have delivered a perfectly healthy baby ten weeks prematurely on a hunch when all she had was a tummy upset from a dodgy meal.'

He sighed. 'I know that really, but my heart won't listen. Not when it's breaking for those poor people and their little son—'

His voice cracked and he stopped. She could hear his breathing; he was fighting for control, subduing the waves of pain. She knew because she was doing it too.

'How about a glass of wine?' she suggested a little unsteadily.

'How about a Scotch?'

She turned and smiled understandingly. 'Good idea. It won't change anything, but it might take the edge off it.'

'Maybe,' he agreed.

He stood up and held his hand out to her, and then as she reached his side he slung his arm round her shoulder and hugged her to his side. 'Thanks, Tink,' he murmured.

She smiled up at him. 'Any time. It works both ways, you know, Joe. If you ever need me, you only have to call.'

He was silent for a moment, then his arm tightened. 'Yeah. I'll bear it in mind. Thanks.'

'Any time. Remember that.'

He swallowed. 'How about that Scotch?'

He let her go, and she lifted her hand and laid it against the tears he had shed against her heart, and wondered if it was possible to love him even more. . .

CHAPTER TEN

THEA thought she would feel different about the job after the tragedy of the James baby. In fact she felt even more privileged after every normal delivery, even more thankful that it had gone well, and rather than toughening her up it had turned her into even more of a marshmallow.

Joe teased her when he caught her with over-bright eyes, but she noticed that his were not always quite as dry as he might lead everyone to believe.

It was a side of him she loved, a human side that he hardly ever showed. It was as if everyone else were entitled to their emotions but his were kept strictly under wraps. She knew that if she hadn't gone into his study she would never have seen him grieve for the lost baby, would never have known how deeply he had felt that loss, that failure.

She had a feeling that he hadn't wanted her to know and almost resented the fact that she did because it made him vulnerable and he didn't like it one bit.

It might have been that, or it might have been tiredness or pressure from other areas of his job that she wasn't privy to, but after the incident of the baby Joe was more withdrawn at home.

He spent more time in his study, and whenever she and MJ were around she always felt he was irritated by their presence. She started subscribing to some general practice journals, and took to combing the adverts in the back for traineeships that caught her eye.

There were very few that she liked the sound of. For the most part they were in inner cities or similarly depressed areas, or out in the wilds of the North York Moors—come back, Heathcliff, all is forgiven, she thought.

No, wild and woolly didn't appeal, and nor did high-rise crime.

Then an advert appeared for a job in a little town north-east of Lancaster. Near Cumbria, in lovely scenery yet not isolated, close to main road and rail links to London and the rest of the world and yet not overly influenced by them, it sounded perfect. It would be a good place to bring up MJ, and far enough from Joe that she could be miserable in peace without having to see him all the time.

It would give her a year to get over him and to decide whether she wanted to work, and if she got really lucky she might just be offered a partnership at the end. Yes. She'd apply.

She wrote out her letter of application and CV, put them in an envelope, and sent them off, then forgot all about it. She didn't have time to dwell on it, anyway, because they had a sudden run of babies and her needle-work skills were very much in demand.

She had a few simple ventouse deliveries, assisted with more complex ones and then, on her very last day, somehow managed to get herself involved in the most bizarre incident of her medical career to date.

An Italian woman with two previous normal deliveries had decided that she had been cheated because she'd never got to see herself giving birth. When Thea was clerking her, she said, 'I wonder would be all right if my friend video the birth?'

Thea didn't have a clue. What was hospital policy? 'I'll have to check for you, but if we were to say yes it would have to be on the understanding that if we needed to ask the person to leave the room she would do so.'

The woman gave a typically Latin shrug. 'Is a he, and tha's all right. He'd go. I'll get Frederico to ring him.'

'Well, let me check first,' Thea told her, and went and found Jenny.

'Oh, yes, that's fine. Often happens, actually. Just make sure they know to keep out of the way and leave if necessary.'

Thea nodded, went back to the patient and told her the glad tidings, and then informed Bev, who was handling the delivery.

'Oh, no, not another one! I thought it was bad news when I read about video cameras years ago. They've been a thorn in my side ever since. Just remember not to swear and keep your best side to the camera.'

Thea laughed. 'Hopefully you won't need me.'

'Hopefully she won't need me, either. With any luck she'll have it in five minutes and go home. She's only in for six hours.'

However, it was not to be. Concepcion—Thea couldn't believe her name was really Concepcion but apparently it was—played to the gallery with every last ounce of her considerable dramatic talent. She groaned, she wept, she grunted, she waddled back and forth. 'She's even been videoed on the loo!' Bev told Thea. Every last gasp was faithfully recorded for posterity by the hairy youth with the video camera.

'I'm studying the visual arts at college,' he told Thea in one of her lightning visits. 'I'm going to be a film-maker.'

Thea hoped the plots would be better than this one or the lad was doomed to failure. She went and found Joe and told him about it, and he groaned and chuckled. 'Who else is in there?'

'Bev and the boyfriend.'

'Keep it that way. You may find otherwise you end up with her extended family. I remember Concepcion from last time, and she's nothing if not gregarious. In fact I seem to remember we threw half a dozen of them out.'

'Perhaps that's why she's having it recorded—for all the people who aren't allowed to come in with her.'

'Someone needs to tell that woman childbirth isn't a spectator sport,' Joe said drily. 'I think I might just slide off home and let William handle any problems.'

'Coward,' Thea teased.

'Too right—want to come?'

Thea laughed. 'No way—it sounds like fun. I wouldn't miss it for the world!'

In the end Bev didn't get her way because the woman's labour wasn't straightforward, unlike the other two. The baby managed to wriggle—due to the melodramatic shenanigans?—until it was lying in an awkward position, at which point it became stuck and ceased to descend.

Bev called Thea, and Thea took one look, swore very softly in deference to the microphone and went to find Joe.

'Concepcion's got a deep transverse arrest,' she told him.

'Oh, God, what have I done to deserve this?' he groaned. 'Right, I want that video camera out!'

He went into the room and asked the young man to leave, but Concepion rallied and refused to let him go. 'If things is goin' wrong, I want the film!' she stated flatly. 'He stays.'

Joe said something the medical defence union would have had trouble defending, but, recognising the futility of argument and not wishing to end up like King Canute with egg on his face, he shrugged, scrubbed and gowned and waded into the fray.

'Just keep out of my way,' he said to the young man, who backed off an inch or two.

Joe examined Concepcion, his eyes trained on the wall behind her as his fingers explored the problem. 'Hmm, it's well stuck, isn't it?' he muttered.

'Could you move over a bit? I can't see,' the young Spielberg said.

Joe withered him with a look and another phrase the medical defence union would have had trouble with, and turned back to his task. 'I'll need the ventouse, I think, Thea, rather than forceps, but it's a bit high. I may have to do an episiotomy. We'll start with a pudendal block to deaden the nerves just to be on the safe side, I think.'

A nurse produced the injection of local anaesthetic and handed it to Joe, who proceeded to inject it into the area around the main nerve supplying the most vulnerable areas. As he did so Concepcion screamed theatrically for the camera, and the young man, Neil, zoomed in on her face.

Joe muttered something inaudible but probably not very flattering, waited the requisite length of time for the pudendal block to take effect and then picked up the episiotomy scissors.

'Hey, Neil, you got a zoom on that machine?'

'Yeah, sure.'

'Zoom on this, then—I'd hate the family to miss it.' He tucked the scissors inside her perineum and Thea heard the familiar sound, 'like scissors cutting raw fish', as one patient had described it to her.

She caught the camera just before Neil hit the ground. Joe turned his head, checked that nothing untoward was happening on the floor and turned back to his job. Concepcion's husband was hovering uncertainly near her head, and Thea handed him the camera. 'Here,' she said. 'She'll kill you if you miss this next bit.'

She moved him down to the end of the delivery table where Concepcion was now propped up in stirrups, and watched as Joe struggled to get the suction cup of the ventouse far enough up to attach to the baby's head.

It was stuck too high, though, and the woman screamed and rolled her eyes, pausing long enough to turn to her husband. 'Frederico, film this! I take you to court! You killing me! Ooh!'

Joe sighed, rolled his own eyes and turned to Thea. 'Your hands are smaller—want to try?'

She grinned weakly. 'And have my fumblings on record for posterity? Do I have to?'

He stepped back. 'Yes. You do. That's an order.'

'You just don't want to be sued,' she hissed under her breath.

'You guessed! Well, come on, we haven't got all day!'

So she changed her gloves and wriggled her fingers about and thought for sure she'd do the woman permanent damage, and then at last she managed to position the cup. They turned the suction on low, gave an experimental tug and it held.

'Hallelujah!' Joe said softly. 'OK, let's get this baby out of there.'

He pulled and turned and wriggled the ventouse and swore a bit and tugged and wriggled some more, and through it all Concepcion yodelled and berated him and exhorted Frederico to make sure he got it all on film, and then suddenly the baby's head shifted and freed, and without any further ado slithered happily down the last few inches and within moments was delivered, followed seconds later by the rest of the gloriously angry little girl.

'*Santa Maria, grazie, molte grazie,*' Concepcion whispered, and burst into her first genuine tears.

Bev handed her the baby and she cradled it lovingly, crooning to it, the camera quite forgotten, then she turned to Joe with a smile that lit her face through the tears. 'Oh, Mr Armitage, thank you! You wonderful man, you know that? You save my baby's life!'

'What an end to my obstetrics career!' Thea said with a laugh.

Joe chuckled. 'At least it was colourful—and a success. You should ask for a copy of the video to put with your CV.'

Thea's face lost its smile. Well, here was her opportunity to raise the subject... 'Yes. Um—I've been meaning to talk to you about that. I've had a call asking me to go for an interview next week—trainee with a country practice. He's going to ring you tonight and talk to you about me.'

'Well, that's great!' He searched her face. 'Isn't it?'

She pulled herself together. 'Oh, yes—yes, I hope so. It looked nice—the right sort of place to bring up a child. I thought I could buy a pleasant little house for us—'

'But you don't need to do that, Thea. You can stay here.'

'No, I can't, Joe. Not indefinitely. You've got a life to lead. We're in your way—'

'No. You're never in my way.'

Thea sighed and pushed her hair back off her face. 'Joe, we are. We crowd you and make you irritable—'

'Irritable? When am I irritable?'

'Often. And anyway, it's much too far.'

'Too far? How can it be too far? Where is it, for God's sake?'

'Near Lancaster.'

His face lost all its colour. 'Lancaster?' he said in disbelief. 'Thea, that's hundreds of miles away.'

She looked down at her hands, knotted together in her lap. 'I know. I wanted to get right out of your way. You've been wonderful to me, Joe, but I think you've more than discharged the debt you felt you owed me. I have to stand on my own feet now—and anyway, you're getting too attached to MJ and he to you. It isn't a good idea.'

'Why not?' he demanded.

'Because when you get married,' she explained patiently, 'your wife won't want someone else's child hanging around you all the time.'

Joe stared at her for a moment, then turned away, stabbing his hand through the rumpled strands of his hair. 'What wife?' he said in a strangled voice. 'There is no wife.'

Her voice softened and she laid her hand on his arm. 'But there will be, one day—sooner if I'm not here to confuse the issue.'

He pulled his arm away. 'Maybe I want the issue confused.'

'Don't be silly. You're only being kind. I know we're in your way—every time you catch me feeding MJ you look embarrassed and I feel awkward about it, and I know you'd rather we weren't here. It's just your stupid pride—'

'You've never embarrassed me, Thea.'

'Yes, I have.'

'No, you haven't!'

'I have, but I don't know why. You never seem to mind at the hospital, or with other women. Why me?'

'Because it's you, damn it! Because it's you, and I— Oh, hell!'

She stared at him. 'You what? You still think of me as your little sister and it doesn't seem right?'

There was an endless silence.

'Because I want you.'

His words dropped into the quiet kitchen like a bombshell.

Thea stepped back, her hand at her throat. Joe wanted her?

'I've never been embarrassed. Ashamed, perhaps.' He drew in a deep breath and let it out in a gust, then turned towards her. 'There's something you maybe ought to know. I wasn't going to tell you because I knew it would change our relationship for ever, but if you're going all the way to Lancaster I can't see it makes much difference.'

He looked down at his hands. 'The reason I look embarrassed is because I'm ashamed of my reaction. There you are, a widow, for God's sake, feeding your baby—an act which is beautiful, a miracle, sacrosanct even—and it turns me on. I despise myself for it, but I can't seem to help it. My eyes are drawn to you, against my will, and I fantasise—'

He looked her in the eye, and his were burning. 'I fantasise that I take the baby from you and lie him down, then lead you to our room and make love to you, suckling from you as the baby has, only there's a difference. You don't look at me as you look at MJ. You look at me with those wide brown eyes and you want me too—'

'I do.'

He froze. 'What?' he choked.

'I do want you. I love you, Joe. I've loved you for years—for ever, almost. Living with you like this has just made it a hundred times worse. I've been pretending, like you—making up little fantasies about us being married, playing house, forgetting that it all had to come to an end—'

'It doesn't have to. You could stay for ever.'

The phone rang, shrill in the background. With a muttered curse Joe picked it up. 'Armitage,' he snapped.

His eyes locked with hers. 'Yes, it is. Can you hold on a moment, please?' He held out the receiver. 'It's the Lion Lane Medical Centre—Dr Matthews. What do I tell him, Thea? Are you staying or going?'

Thea's heart was racing, threatening to burst out of her chest. 'What are you asking me, Joe?' she prompted.

'To stay. To marry me. To be my wife.'

She chewed her lip. 'But why?'

'Because I love you, dammit, and I won't let you go to Lancaster without me!'

She let her breath out in a whoosh. 'Then I'd better marry you, hadn't I?'

Their eyes held, and he reached for her, hooking the phone off the worktop onto the floor.

Thea backed away. 'Hadn't you better put him out of his misery?' she said with a smile. 'This could take some time.'

He grinned—a slow, sexy grin that melted her insides—and lifted the receiver to his ear. 'Um—sorry about this. There's been a change of plan.' He looked up and met her eyes. 'Thank you. Thank you very much. Yes, I'll tell her.' He picked the phone up, put it together and dumped it on the worktop. 'He heard. He said congratulations. He also said he was very disappointed and if you changed your mind and decided I wasn't worth the effort, get in touch. He liked your letter.'

Thea laughed softly. 'Oh, dear. Well, he'll be disappointed. It's taken me twenty years to get you to this point, Joe. I'm not going to let you go now.'

He laughed a little raggedly and tugged her into his arms. 'Oh, Thea—I thought I was going to have to spend the next however many years pretending to be your brother just to keep you near me—'

His voice cracked, and his arms tightened around her, drawing her even closer to his heart. 'I love you, Thea,' he muttered into her hair. 'I know I'm not Mike but I'll do everything I can to make you happy.'

'I don't want you to be Mike,' she said softly. 'Mike's dead. I loved him, I did what I could for him but it was never like this, Joe, eating me alive inside.' She tipped back her head. 'Make love to me, Joe,' she whispered.

His eyes slid shut, veiling the raging need she glimpsed in them. 'MJ's crying,' he grated. 'Feed him first.'

He let her go, and she went up to the baby's room and lifted him out of his cot, Joe hard on her heels. 'Hello, sweetheart,' she murmured. 'Are you thirsty?'

The baby whimpered and reached for her T-shirt, pulling it out of his way, and Joe gave a strained chuckle. 'He knows what he wants.'

She looked up with a smile. 'It must be the role model.'

Joe was ignoring her. His eyes were on the baby, his greedy mouth fastened on her nipple, the tiny hand resting on the pale, blue-veined curve above.

And Thea watched Joe, his eyes fixed on her without shame now, without need to hide his feelings, and she felt her body quiver like a bowstring. His skin was drawn tight over his cheekbones, his mouth parted slightly, his chest moving visibly with his rapid breathing. As she watched, his tongue flicked out to moisten his lips, and her breath caught in her throat.

The baby went to sleep, his thirst satisfied, and Thea handed him to Joe. Her hands shook like leaves in the breeze, and her voice felt unused and strained. 'Put him down for me,' she whispered.

Joe laid him carefully in his cot—very carefully, so as not to wake him, and then he straightened.

'Thea?'

She reached out her hand, and he took it, drawing her to his side. 'I need you,' he whispered rawly. 'Now. Please.'

Thea's legs buckled, and he swept her up into his arms and carried her through to his bedroom, kicking the door

shut behind him. Then he set her down in the centre of
the bed and knelt beside her. Her T-shirt was still hitched
up, caught on the damp nipple, and Joe pushed it aside
and bent his head. His tongue flicked over the puckered
tip and a shudder ran through her. He groaned and drew
the nipple deep into his mouth, suckling hard, and a
sobbing cry ripped from her throat.

How could it be so different? Her hands knotted in
his hair, clutching him against her, aching for more. He
cupped her other breast, smoothing her bra aside, chafing
the nipple with the flattened palm, and she whimpered
his name.

His head lifted, his eyes burning with a blue flame
that scorched her with its heat.

'Sit up,' he ordered gruffly.

She sat, and he peeled her T-shirt off over her head
and then pulled off her dangling bra. His eyes tracked
over her and closed. 'Dear God, you are so lovely.' His
throat worked convulsively, and she reached for him, her
fingers fumbling with the buttons of his shirt.

He couldn't wait. The shirt was gone, ripped over his
head in a shower of flying buttons, then he pushed her
down and lifted her hips, stripping off her leggings and
leaving her just the scant protection of her serviceable
cotton briefs. His finger slid under the elastic and traced
round the leg, across the sensitive skin of her abdomen
and down over the tangle of curls that shielded her most
wild imaginings.

'Joe,' she pleaded, and he smiled, no longer in a hurry.

She was, though. He was kneeling up beside her and
she reached for the belt on his jeans and yanked it undone,
then found herself defeated by the stud. 'Help me, damn

it!' she muttered, and he laughed softly and opened the stud.

Her fingers hooked over the waistband and slid round, over the hard washboard of his lean abdomen. Her fingertips grazed the hard bulge that the jeans could scarcely contain and he sucked his breath in and caught her hand. 'Easy,' he breathed.

She didn't want to take it easy. She wanted it—him—now. She looked up into her eyes. 'Please, Joe, don't tease me. I need you.'

His eyes widened, flaring with white-hot passion, and then he was beside her, shucking his jeans off and stripping away first his briefs, then hers, his lean, hard thigh moving between hers to nudge her knees apart. His hand slid down over her hip and round, cupping the terrifying ache only he could cure, and his mouth locked with hers in a kiss that left her breathless and sobbing.

'Joe,' she whimpered. 'Please—now. . .'

Then he was there, his body moving over hers, surging into her as she opened for him like a flower in the morning sun. He stiffened, his body shuddering, and then he lifted his head and looked deep into her eyes.

'Look at me, Thea,' he whispered roughly. 'I want you to know it's me.'

Her eyes filled with tears. 'Oh, Joe, I know it's you. I know it's you, my darling.'

A harsh breath shook him, and he dropped his head into her shoulder. 'Damn. I wanted this to last for you.'

Her arms cradled him. 'Oh, Joe. Just love me.'

'I do,' he murmured. 'You know I do.'

And then he moved, his body coiled like a spring, filling her time and time again, until his control slipped and with a muttered oath he drove into her, harder and harder, winding her tighter with every stroke, until with a sudden cry she was free.

'Joe!' she sobbed, and then his body arched against her, her name ripped from his throat in a harsh cry, then again, softly, like a vow.

'Thea. . .'

He fell against her, his breath rasping in his throat, his heart pounding with hers, and she smoothed her hands over his sweat-slicked skin and pressed a kiss to his hair.

He levered himself up and fell beside her, pulling her into his arms, his body drained of energy. It must be, she thought dimly, after that. So much power released so fast. . . She laid her hand against his heart, threading her fingers through the fine scatter of hairs, and felt the beat gradually slow and steady.

'Wow,' she murmured.

His arm tightened round her, and she felt his chest shake with laughter. 'That was an understatement,' he mumbled.

Thea chuckled and lifted herself up to look down at him. The fire had burned down in his eyes, and in its place was a tender warmth that bathed her in happiness.

'I think it's time I told you about Mike,' she said, and the warmth faded, leaving a bleak emptiness.

'Not now, Thea,' he pleaded.

'Yes, now. Joe, he was just a friend. I cared for him, got to know him, spent time with him, and he fell in love with me. I didn't love him, not like this, not like I love you, but he didn't turn me off, either.' She touched his cheek, turning his face back to hers. 'Our lovemaking was pleasant, but not spectacular. We didn't set the room on fire. It was just a part of our relationship, and it was little enough to give him with so short a time left. Anyway, I could never regret it, because of the baby.' She pressed a kiss to his hand.

'He's the only other man I've ever slept with, and without him, without MJ, I wouldn't be here with you now, so I can't allow myself any regrets. I just don't want you hurting because you imagine I'm grief-stricken over Mike. I don't want there to be any doubt in your mind that you aren't just my second choice. If you'd been in my life when I met Mike, I wouldn't have given him another glance, but you weren't. I was alone, and so was he, and it didn't seem so much to give.'

Joe took her hand and pressed it to his lips. 'I don't suppose you have any idea what you gave him. What holding you, sharing his fears with you, having you by his side could actually have meant.'

He met her eyes, and his were bright with tears. 'When you were seven or eight—shortly after I came to your family—you came to see me one night to tell me what you'd been doing. You were supposed to be having a bath, and you sat in my room, on the end of my bed, and chattered to me for ages. Then your mother called you, and you slipped off the bed and ran to the door, and then you changed your mind for some reason and came back to me, and you put your arms round me and kissed me, and told me you loved me.'

She laughed self-consciously. 'I remember. You were so embarrassed you went all stiff and funny.'

'I was holding a handful of sleeping pills,' he told her. 'They were your mother's, left from when she'd been ill, and I'd stolen them and was going to take them.'

Thea sat up and stared at him, the shock stealing her breath. 'Joe?' she whispered, her eyes wide. 'You were so young! Far too young to die!'

'There was nothing to live for,' he said quietly. 'Not until you said that, and I sat for a while and thought about how you would feel if I killed myself, and I went and flushed them down the loo.'

Tears flooded over her cheeks and she blinked them away. 'But you could have died.' She reached for him, her eyes flooding again. 'Oh, Joe, I could have lost you for ever.'

He folded her against his chest and she lay there trembling, listening to the steady, reassuring beat of his heart and wondering how she could have borne it if he'd died.

'No,' she whispered.

'I couldn't do it to you, Thea. I could do it to me, or to your parents, but not to you. You were the only sunshine in my life, the only warmth, the only truly decent thing to happen to me in ages. I couldn't destroy you.'

'It would have done,' she said with absolute certainty.

'I know. And that was my debt, Thea. My life. I owed you for my life, and nothing would have been too great a sacrifice, even if, God forbid, it meant I had to live with you and pretend to be your brother for the rest of my days.'

His hand cupped her cheek, and she felt him tremble. 'I owe you everything, Thea, my life, my happiness— everything. I don't think you can have any idea what your love means to me.'

His lips found hers, gentle and undemanding, and with a sigh she took him in her arms and drew him down to her. Their lovemaking was tender, slow and unhurried this time, the urgency gone, and Joe staked his claim on every last clamouring inch of her body.

By the time he had reached her toes she was mindless with need for him, and with a throaty chuckle of satisfaction he moved over her, teasing her again, tormenting her, until with a sob of exasperation she wrapped her legs round him and drew him, willing, into the haven of her body.

He teased her even then, until the tendrils of passion coiled round him and drew him into the boiling maelstrom of their shattering release.

'Joe?'

'Mmm?'

'MJ's crying.'

'Mmm.'

She pushed him with her foot. 'Well, go on, then.'

He rolled out of bed, grumbling gently, and stumbled across the room in the darkness. He found the landing light, then, blinking in the glare, he went into the baby's room.

MJ was standing in his cot, pulled up on the bars, his little face puckered.

'Shh, son, don't cry,' Joe murmured soothingly. He lifted the little body up against his chest, the small arms circling his neck, and carried him back to his mother.

'What's wrong with him?'

Joe shrugged. 'I don't know. He's stopped crying. Perhaps he needs his nappy changed.'

'Perhaps he just needs a cuddle from his dad.'

Joe's chest contracted. 'I wish he was my son. That used to be part of my fantasy—that he was mine.'

He felt Thea's hand on his arm, her eyes in the dim

light glazed with tears. 'He couldn't be any more yours if he really was,' she said gently. 'Mike never even knew about him, but if he had I'm sure he would have been more than happy to know you would love the baby as your own.'

Joe bent his head and pressed his lips to MJ's baby-soft hair. 'I couldn't love him any more, that's for sure. If we have our own, in the future, they won't be any more precious than him.'

'Oh, Joe—' Thea broke off, her voice clogged with tears, and Joe settled himself beside her and pulled her into the crook of his arm. The baby lay on his chest, sleeping again, comforted by their presence, and Joe thought that nothing on earth could be a greater gift than the love of this child and his mother.

'Joe?'

He kissed her head. 'Yes, my love?'

'Would you consider adopting him?'

Joe's chest squeezed even tighter, and his eyes misted. 'How do you think Mike would feel?'

'Proud of him. Happy that he was loved. Sad to miss it all. I'd want MJ to know all about his natural father, but you'll always be his real father, the man he turns to, the one who's here for him. I think it would be right that he was legally your child.'

Joe took a steadying breath and tried to shift the lump in his throat. 'Hell, Thea—' he began, but his voice cracked.

She smoothed his cheek, brushing away the tears. 'Was that a yes?'

He laughed, a little raggedly. 'Yes. It was a yes. . .'

*　　*　　*

The baby wriggled down, sliding between them and ending up curled against the soft curve of Thea's tummy. Her hand stroked his cheek and he slept again, his head against her.

Deep within his mother, mere inches from the baby's head, another miracle was beginning—a little girl for Joe to call his own. . .

MILLS & BOON®

Medical Romance™

COMING NEXT MONTH

A MIDWIFE'S CHALLENGE by Frances Crowne

Katy Woods resolved never to get involved with men after her disastrous marriage to a bigamist—until she met Dr Mark Hammond. He was irresistible—until she discovered the truth about his ex-girlfriend, which was a haunting reminder of her past...

FULL RECOVERY by Lilian Darcy

Camberton Hospital

Helen Darnell suspected her husband of twenty years, Nick, to be having an affair with a beautiful doctor. Helen tried to quell her fears believing that Nick was faithful to her. Their marriage was teetering on the edge of destruction and only one thing could save it—the truth.

DOCTOR ACROSS THE LAGOON by Margaret Holt

Lucinda Hallcross-Spriggs' journey to Italy for a medical conference took an unexpected turn when she met the devilishly handsome Dr Pino Ponti. She soon succumbed to his relentless charm, but with his restless heart and uneasy past, she surely had no part to play in his future.

LAKELAND NURSE by Gill Sanderson

Zanne Ripley's application for Medical School was unsuccessful—and all because of Dr Neil Calder. Now she had to work with him at the Mountain Activities Centre, but his charm soon broke down her defences. But Neil had a secret...

'Happy' Greetings!

Would you like to win a year's supply of Mills & Boon® books? Well you can and they're free! Simply complete the competition below and send it to us by 31st August 1997. The first five correct entries picked after the closing date will each win a year's subscription to the Mills & Boon series of their choice. What could be easier?

ACSPPMTHYHARSI

‗ ‗ ‗ ‗ ‗ ‗ ‗ ‗ ‗ ‗ ‗ ‗ ‗

TPHEEYPSARA

‗ ‗ ‗ ‗ ‗ ‗ ‗ ‗ ‗ ‗ ‗

RAHIHPYBDYTAP

‗ ‗ ‗ ‗ ‗ ‗ ‗ ‗ ‗ ‗ ‗ ‗ ‗

NHMYRTSPAAPNERUY

‗ ‗ ‗ ‗ ‗ ‗ ‗ ‗ ‗ ‗ ‗ ‗ ‗ ‗ ‗ ‗

DYVLTEPYAANINSEPAH

‗ ‗ ‗ ‗ ‗ ‗ ‗ ‗ ‗ ‗ ‗ ‗ ‗ ‗ ‗ ‗ ‗ ‗

YAYPNAHPEREW

‗ ‗ ‗ ‗ ‗ ‗ ‗ ‗ ‗ ‗ ‗ ‗

DMHPYAHRYOSETPA

‗ ‗ ‗ ‗ ‗ ‗ ‗ ‗ ‗ ‗ ‗ ‗ ‗ ‗ ‗

VRHYPNARSAEYNPIA

‗ ‗ ‗ ‗ ‗ ‗ ‗ ‗ ‗ ‗ ‗ ‗ ‗ ‗ ‗ ‗

Please turn over for details of how to enter ☞

How to enter...

There are eight jumbled up greetings overleaf, most of which you will probably hear at some point throughout the year. Each of the greetings is a 'happy' one, i.e. the word 'happy' is somewhere within it. All you have to do is identify each greeting and write your answers in the spaces provided. Good luck!

When you have unravelled each greeting don't forget to fill in your name and address in the space provided and tick the Mills & Boon® series you would like to receive if you are a winner. Then simply pop this page into an envelope (you don't even need a stamp) and post it today. Hurry—competition ends 31st August 1997.

Mills & Boon 'Happy' Greetings Competition
FREEPOST, Croydon, Surrey, CR9 3WZ

Please tick the series you would like to receive if you are a winner

Presents™ ❑ Enchanted™ ❑ Medical Romance™ ❑
Historical Romance™ ❑ Temptation® ❑

Are you a Reader Service Subscriber? Yes ❑ No ❑

Ms/Mrs/Miss/Mr _____

(BLOCK CAPS PLEASE)

Address _____

_____

_____ Postcode _____

(I am over 18 years of age)

One application per household. Competition open to residents of the UK and Ireland only.

You may be mailed with other offers from other reputable companies as a result of this application. If you would prefer not to receive such offers, please tick box. ❑

C7B

mps MAILING PREFERENCE SERVICE DMA